USA TODAY BESTSELLING AUTHOR

KEL CARPENTER

INFERNAL DESIRES

QUEEN OF THE DAMNED BOOK THREE

Created with Vellum

To strong women who simply can't be contained, you inspire me.

"Just gonna stand there and watch me burn / that's alright because I like the way it hurts."

~ Eminem and Rihanna, *Love The Way You Lie*

CHAPTER 1

I was on fire.

At least it felt that way as I turned from the wall of glass that left all of New Orleans on display. The city of the dead. We were at Hell's motherfucking gates, and what happens?

I started the transition.

How long did Rysten say I had before it fully set in? Forty-eight hours? And then what?

I shivered and it sure as hell wasn't because I was cold. I was half-succubus and half...the beast. Pre-transition, I burned down Blue Ruby Ink. I branded Laran *and* Moira. I shredded the nightmare imp's soul. And I've nearly fucked all of the Horsemen but one.

So...what would I do during the transition? Would it even be me—or would it be the beast?

I sighed roughly, running a sweaty hand through my hair.

This was all assuming I didn't spontaneously combust into flames by then.

"Everything alright, love?" Rysten asked, pulling me back to reality. I blinked away the haziness to see him standing in the doorway.

"You said I have forty-eight hours. What happens then?" I asked, my throat already dry and scratchy. I took another step toward him and stopped abruptly when I felt a shift in the air. It was almost undetectable. His eyes dilated and he shut them, inhaling deeply.

And when he opened his eyes, it wasn't the Rysten I knew and cared for.

I blinked as a mist formed around him. Individual flecks of white formed on his skin. Gathering and condensing as they slowly built, it fell around him like snow...or ash. Oddly beautiful. Terrifyingly strange.

"Are you seeing this..." my words trailed off as he took another shuddering breath. He let out a groan.

"So sweet," he murmured.

I frowned, narrowing my eyes. The mist shifted and swirled around him, twisting and pulsing in sync with something. *His heart.*

"What happens then?" Those three little words came out far more seductive than I thought possible. I took a step closer and Rysten's eyes darkened from green to nearly black, but not with rage. With...

"Either your succubus nature or the beast will take over. Possibly both." His tongue darted out, licking his bottom lip. The heat inside me climbed ever higher. Pretty soon I was going to be at risk of passing out. Maybe that was for the best, considering the look Rysten was giving me.

"And then?" I asked hoarsely, my voice no more than a whisper. He smiled, but there was nothing boyish or cute about it. A feral look had entered his eye, that of a predator with only one purpose.

"You will need to feed." He took three steps towards me before my brain realized what he was doing. The haze was already starting to descend again. The pulsing heat inside, guiding me towards it. Towards him.

"What are you doing?" I whispered through chapped lips. My legs shook the closer he came, and I wasn't sure if it was exertion or need. Even in his scary as fuck state, I was incapable of feeling truly afraid. He wouldn't hurt me.

Rysten crossed the distance between us with measured steps. By the time he was standing before me, his eyes were completely black. Not a trace of any color in sight.

I bit my lip, simultaneously fighting the urge to lean into him and to faint. Rysten made my choice easy, reaching out and wrapping a strong arm completely around my waist. He gripped my hip, claw-tipped fingers biting into the skin just beneath my thick sweater. I let out a low moan and breathed deeply.

His scent hit me like a freight train and I wrapped both my hands in the material of his shirt. Rysten took that as all the invitation he needed. He reached up with his other hand and buried it in my hair, using his hold to guide my head back. My body turned to Jell-O at his touch as the burning inside me grew out of control, seeking some sort of release.

He brought his lips to mine and every thought vanished.

I simply couldn't think, couldn't feel anything beyond his lips as they melded to mine. He kissed me with such passion that I was blindsided by lust. Consumed by it.

Enough so that I didn't think twice when he dropped one arm from my waist to my ass and hoisted me up. I wrapped my legs around him without needing to be told. The hard bulge in his pants rubbed against me, causing a frenzy to set in.

I placed my hands on his shoulders, relishing in the hard, corded muscle I found there. My fingers teased his collar, dipping inside his shirt before my impatience got the better of me. My fingers wrapped around the thick fabric and pulled. Buttons popped as I ripped his shirt down the middle. My hands flattened over the smooth skin of his chest. He growled in approval, making my stomach flutter. Inside, the flames fanned hotter.

My back touched cool glass, clearing my head just enough to know this wasn't normal. I may be a bit horny more often than I liked to admit, but I didn't usually jump someone's bones in two seconds flat. I pulled back from our kiss to breathe and ask him what the hell was going on. Rysten used that brief half a second to grind into me, trailing a delicious row of kisses and bites down my neck.

My head lolled back, resting against the glass while arching my back to give him better access to *everything*, because in that moment nothing else mattered. Only the burning within and between us that kept me in a hazy reality where the only thing that made sense was his skin on mine.

"What the—"

The sudden interruption was loud enough to register but not enough to permeate the blazing heat that gripped me. One moment I was pressed against the glass, and the next I was on my hands and knees.

A savage snarl escaped my lips as I looked up at the two Horsemen that restrained Rysten, his pitch black demon eyes locked on mine.

"You're a fucking idiot," War snapped at him. He moved to put Rysten in a headlock and Death let him. I let out a warning growl of my own as outrage took hold of me and acted. It didn't even occur to me that the beast was goading me into it until after I shoved Julian out of the way and bitch-slapped Laran.

I stopped dead in my tracks as the haze cleared again and dread formed in my stomach. Laran stood stock-still, gaping at me as he dropped Rysten like a lead weight. Whatever trance-like lust seemed to have fallen over him snapped the moment he hit the ground. His eyes cleared, turning back to a vivid dark green as the ivory mist around him evaporated.

I shook my head, trying to make sense of the craziness.

"Ruby, love, I am *so* sorry—" His apology broke off when Laran kicked him in the head.

"Hey!" I snapped at Laran, the spiraling rage that started this all leapt to the forefront again. "What the hell, Laran?" My fists clenched on their own accord, but I kept myself from taking a swing.

"Ruby," Julian said in a deceptively soft tone, "do you realize your hands are on fire?"

I dared a glance at my hands to see that blue fire did indeed consume them. The tendrils skated up my arms, as high as my elbows, but didn't burn.

I swallowed hard again and grit my teeth, willing the fire to go out.

Of course, it wasn't that simple.

At first, nothing happened. It didn't shrink, but it also didn't grow. In some ways, I called that a win. After all, almost every time I've used the flames, someone has either died or a building burned down. So in some ways, nothing happening was an improvement.

Until my clothes caught.

"For fuck's sake," I groaned, turning to the beast inside me. She extinguished the flames without making me ask, but I didn't miss the vicious smile that followed. The beast knew what was going on here. That very soon I would have little to no control.

In a matter of days there would be no one to truly stand between the beast and the world.

No one except the Horsemen, that is.

I guess it's a good thing this was what they were created for, because looking after me is turning out to be a full-time job.

CHAPTER 2

I STEPPED AROUND LARAN WITH A HUFF, STRIDING down the hallway. Moira stood in the doorway, bent over at the waist, laughing so hard she swayed sideways and bumped into me. I rolled my eyes and grabbed her arm, hauling her into the bedroom behind me before slamming the door shut. It wouldn't keep the Horsemen away forever, but it might give me a few minutes reprieve.

The door pounded behind me.

"For the love of—" I cracked the door, but Julian was the one I least expected to find.

"Ruby, I know this must be—"

"Five minutes. Can I have five fucking minutes to myself?" I snapped. Julian didn't flinch, and he didn't leave.

"With the transition starting in—"

"Rysten said I had forty-eight hours. I'm asking for five minutes." Refusing to back down, I held his gaze before it turned glacial and impassive.

"Fine." The muscle in his jaw ticked. I moved to shut the door, but he caught it with his hand. "If I hear anything—"

"Five. Minutes," I repeated, pushing against the door. It didn't budge until he pulled away, giving me a tight nod as he did.

The door clicked shut and I turned, leaning back and resting my head against it. Staring at the ceiling, I finally got the nerve to say, "What am I going to do?"

"Same thing you always do," Moira said. I rocked my body forward, pushing off the door. My gaze dropped to my best friend as I cocked an eyebrow in her direction, silently asking what that was. She pursed her lips and said one word. "Survive."

Bandit walked over to me and tugged my jeans. I leaned over and scooped him up in my arms, walking over to sit on the white feather comforter. Moira joined us, sprawling out beside me.

"I'm scared," I whispered into his fur. He purred, nuzzling against me.

"Of course you are," she scoffed. "I'd be worried if you weren't." Moira arched up to tuck both her arms behind her head like she didn't have a care in the world. She did, but it was only my empathic abilities and years of watching her that told me so. "But you have me," she continued, very self-important-like. "And the trash panda *and* the Horsemen. At least part of them, when they're not trying to fuck you." She snickered and Bandit let out this god-awful rasping sound. I splayed a hand over my forehead, swiping it down my face, letting out an exasperated sigh.

"That's what I'm worried about," I muttered. "What if the Horsemen can't stop me? What if—" I paused, steeling myself to tell her the truth. To say my next words. "What if the beast emerges and I end up killing everyone in New Orleans?"

Moira seemed to ruminate on her response, sucking the air between her teeth before replying, "I don't think it will come to that."

I squinted at the ceiling, tilting my head. "How do you figure that?"

"Two reasons. The first is that all four of those lazy fuckers have a raging hard-on for you. I thought Julian was going to bend your ass over and fuck you there when you started growling at them all come-hither-like on your hands and knees," she chuckled again.

"I did not—"

"Oh yes you did," she smirked, wagging her finger. "Save the modesty for someone else. You've been my best friend for over ten years. I know what you're like when you get horny and can't fuck. Hello, welcome to the past five years."

I rolled my eyes, arching to grab the pillow from underneath me to chuck it at her face. She caught it without missing a beat.

"The second reason," she said with exaggerated slowness, "is because you're a succubus that's been starving for over five years. Something tells me your transition is going to be one hell of show." She grinned, the blue pentagrams in her eyes swirling around mischievously.

"Please tell me you are not planning to watch—"

"Fuck no." She made a gagging noise that descended

into giggles. "I love you, Rubes, but you're like my sister. Your transition is one porno I am not interested in watching. If I want to get it on, Bourbon Street isn't far."

Bourbon Street. The one place on this continent that you could throw a rock blindfolded and be more likely to hit a demon than a human. Only three blocks from Hell's Gates, it was practically overrun with our kind. Which meant it wasn't safe for me or for her, not with those glowing blue-branded eyes.

She wore the Devil's mark, and if her glamour slipped for even a second, it was all over. The world would know that a new soul carried that name.

"Please tell me you're not planning on going down to Bourbon Street with everything that's going on..." I said. She inclined her head and wariness permeated the air. "Moira, you can't be serious." She let out a sigh.

"I wouldn't say planning is the right word. More like *considering* my options," she defended. "It's not like anyone is going to cross over until you transition. Once you fully hit it, that could be weeks. It would be a shame for me to miss out on the chance before we left earth..."

I know she didn't mean for it to come across like she was guilt-tripping me, but her subtle reminder pulled at my heartstrings. Both because this is entirely on me, and because I almost lost her once. Despite that, she chose to follow me, and not just to the ends of this world, but to another world entirely.

I sat up, ignoring Bandit's protests as I moved him aside and embraced her, wrapping my arms around her petite frame. "I'm not going to tell you what you can and can't do. I just worry about you," I whispered into her dark green hair. She smelled like mint and spring.

"I know." She wrapped her arms around my waist, holding me tight against her. "It's the same for me. I've never worried about anyone or anything in my life until you, and I'm not even getting some," she grumbled. "Which is why I'm *thinking* about it, but my mind isn't made up. You know I'd never do anything that puts you in danger."

"It's not me I'm worried about."

A knock at the door interrupted us and I growled under my breath. Moira clutched me tighter, shaking with silent laughter as the door swung open.

"Ruby, love, I hate to break this up, but Allistair will be here shortly and we need to talk about how you want to do this."

I could only assume he meant go through the transition, to which I didn't have an answer. Still, I unclasped myself from Moira and followed him back out into the living room.

He took a seat in the lone armchair across the room, shooting me an apologetic look. I briefly wondered if his distance was because of our unexplainable make-out session earlier, or the shattered trust we'd yet to mend from Moira's kidnapping. Judging by Julian's turned back as he faced the glass wall, arms clasped behind him, I could only guess it was some of both.

I took a step towards Laran who sat on the black leather loveseat, freezing when his eyes swept up—hot, heated, and cautious. It was that last one that gave me pause.

"Is something wrong here?" I asked, my voice coming out a bit sharper than I intended, a hint of the beast inside me creeping through. She was not happy with him. Neither of us understood why he, out of any of them, would be wary with us.

He was branded.

He was *ours*.

A heavy fog formed around him, seemingly coming from nowhere. Red as human blood, frothing and foaming as it poured outward from him. I blinked, narrowing my eyes as I cocked my head.

"I asked you a question, Laran." It was not my voice that came out, this was sultry and smooth. Layered with seduction and fire, the words seemed to settle over him. His eyes went wholly black, blotting out any trace of white. My lips parted as heat circled through me, shooting up my veins to that aching place in my core. A pounding started in my head.

I took another step towards him, only mildly aware of the outside voices speaking words that didn't matter. Laran clenched his hands as if trying to restrain himself. From what, I didn't know, but the pounding urged me closer, pushing me towards him.

I moved to stand directly between his legs, reaching forward through the fog—

Strong hands wrapped around my waist, yanking me back, pulling me away from him. From my—

"Snap out of it, Ruby," a voice, rough and thick with desire, whispered in my ear. I stepped back into something solid. My lips parted on their own accord, tasting the air around me. Lust and heat. Darkness and shadows.

12

Cold so chilling that it ignited a burning desire going down my lungs, straight to that place between my thighs.

The body behind me stayed still as the dead, neither pulling me closer nor releasing me to the world. Like he was having trouble making up his mind. I reached my arms up and around behind me, gripping his shoulders. My fingers trailed across his taut muscles, sweeping up the bare skin of his neck, and twining around short locks of hair that I knew would be white. I gave a sharp tug, smiling as a growl escaped his composure.

The hands at my waist tightened, almost painfully so, but he did not budge.

"Do not test me," Death whispered in my ear. His lips were chilled as they brushed down the nape of my neck and up again. He inhaled deeply and I shuddered in delight. "Hell's heir, you may be, but no one courts Death unless they wish to *submit*."

My control was already hanging on by a very thin thread. The image that swept through my mind of him dominating me snapped it entirely. The beast pushed forward and ground my hips back into the hard erection that pressed against me.

The breath hissed between his teeth.

"Death, you may be, but you will kneel all the same," my beast replied. Her version of kneel looked nothing like what most imagined. She didn't just want his submission. She wanted his adoration, his devotion, his very fucking soul.

Her idea of Death kneeling ended with his face between my thighs and my mark branded on his fucking cock.

Oh man, I was so utterly screwed.

But I couldn't bring myself to stop it.

Heat burned through me like a building inferno. Pounding. Beating. Pushing me towards something that I didn't fully understand. I pushed back, running my ass over the length of him—

Crack!

I blinked. Not that I was opposed to pain, but I found it rather unexpected. My vision cleared, and it was not Death or any of the Horsemen standing in front of me, but Moira.

She arched one dark green eyebrow, her arms folded over her chest smugly.

"I know you are horny as fuck right now, but there is a time and place, and it is not in front of my not-so-virgin eyes. Get it together, Rubes."

My beast blinked at her.

"Did you just slap me?" the beast asked, frowning in confusion. Moira didn't back down.

"Yes. You're a thirsty bitch. I get it. But I need you to hold yourself together just a little bit longer." The beast looked at her, tilting my head, the pounding in my veins easing for just a moment. "For me. Can you do it for me?" she asked quietly. Not pleading, because Moira never begged. Instead, she was demanding of the beast what no one else in this room could.

Because they were not our tether. The one who kept us together when all else failed.

And for her, we would do anything.

The beast reached out with our hand and swept a

stray lock of her dark green hair aside. Intimate, but not sexual in any way.

"For you, who has protected her always. Be warned: very soon I will not be able to stop." Our head rose as she locked eyes with Laran who sat several feet behind Moira, watching me intensely, his gaze dark. "I will claim *all* my mates before we return home."

With that she receded, leaving me clammy and confused.

I didn't even have time to register the voice behind me before the bright spots in my vision exploded. The world went white as sleep found me, but the fire inside did not abate.

Not even sleep could save me from my infernal torment...or desires.

JULIAN

She had me. She had me, and she *knew* it.

Whereas Ruby and I had danced around her growing attraction to me and the painfully addictive things I felt for her, the beast would not. We'd been chosen, created, to be her protectors, but the beast wanted more.

It wanted all of us. All of me.

She wanted to own every aspect of me. My soul.

At least that creature cared not for whether there was some semblance of a heart left in me, beyond the useless beating thing in my chest. I wouldn't fail her in that regard. She may have been raised human, but the girl in my arms was fire and ash through and through.

Her skin glowed like the embers of a budding flame. Hotter than a star and deadlier than anything this world could imagine, the power she kept within her was rarely present, apart from when she slept. In this state, I could feel her need clawing at me, getting beneath my skin, even more pronounced than when she taunted me.

I cradled her body close to my chest, pretending not to be affected by the way she wrapped her arms around my neck, clinging to me even in sleep. I breathed in the scent of her. The way it called to me.

"We need to move her," Laran said.

I couldn't admit it to them. The way I felt. I couldn't admit it to Ruby herself, even though I knew it pained her for me to deny us both. I wanted her unlike anything or anyone that came before her.

And much as I tried to stay away, for the sake of us all, I was rapidly approaching my breaking point.

"She will need to feed when she wakes," Allistair began. I growled under my breath at the mere thought of it because I wouldn't be the one to do it. "Do you have something to say, Death?"

I held her closer by a fraction of an inch.

Did I have a problem?

I did.

I was far too conflicted about this. If I was doing my damn job, I would hand her over and let it be done. I would refuse her advances. I would deny the mating bond that she's offering.

I would keep her safe and not get distracted. Not dream about the color her skin would turn after meeting my belt, or fantasize the ways she might moan for me.

I would know that the only way this could end, is up in flames.

And yet...I couldn't walk away.

Neither could I admit any of it aloud.

Instead of answering, I walked away, carrying the sleeping she-demon in my arms.

"Hey," the banshee screeched behind me. "What do you think you're doing? Where are you going?"

"Keeping her safe."

It was the only answer I could give. I didn't want to think about what Allistair would do to her. With her. My own possessiveness did not lend to sharing, and if I took her through her first feed...I would brand every inch of her skin.

But Ruby wouldn't want that, and I couldn't stop myself.

Something slammed into my back and crumpled. Not a person, but an object. I turned slightly to see shards of broken glass. A lamp. And the banshee who threw it.

"You don't get to just remove her without answers. I asked you what you were doing, because if you idiots aren't smart, all you'll do is piss her off and if you think I'm bad, you ain't seen nothing yet!" Her words strayed toward a southern twang the more she got worked up.

"Calm yourself," I replied coldly. "The transition is messing with her mind. She will be unable to think logically until she feeds. I'm moving her to a private room that is warded heavily enough for her to do so and not be a danger to the city."

The banshee paused. She didn't trust us, and it was somewhat admirable that she distrusted anyone with her best friend. She truly was a proper familiar. Possessive. Slightly irrational. Distrusting of anyone else's intentions, but entirely loyal to the one who bound her.

It was the only reason she was standing after throwing a lamp at me.

"She's not going to like this."

19

"The alternative is we wait for her to wake and give her a choice, at which point she will either agree to it, or the far more likely option, her anger will again spiral and I will not be able to put her to sleep." Allistair chose to step forward and interject with a more diplomatic understanding of the scenario. "Ruby is the strongest succubus I have seen pre-transition and she is scared to go through it. That is going to make it very difficult on her already. If she burns the city down in a rage, that will only make her more volatile and unstable. This is the best solution."

Her eyes scanned Ruby, softening as she watched her with a weary expression. She didn't like this, but she was out of her depth. We were the Horsemen, and this was what we were meant to do. Familiar or not, the responsibility of ensuring Ruby transitioned safely was on the four of us.

With a nod from the banshee, I turned my back on them and hoped that we were enough.

That we could do just what we'd told her we would, because if not...it wouldn't just be the banshee's anger we would have to answer to.

CHAPTER 3

Shadows danced in the candlelight when I came to. I laid there for a moment, in that strange in-between state where I was awake but not fully, staring at the shades of black and grey as they swayed from side to side. There was something so peaceful about it, but that didn't resonate with me. Not this time. Not with my body wound tight as a spring, coiled and waiting for release.

Where am I?

I rolled over, pausing midway. Lantern-like orbs hung from the ceiling, emitting a soft glow. Tiny, twinkling lights blinked in and out of existence—absorbing me with their simple beauty. I leaned up, reaching for one with an outstretched hand.

"How are you feeling?"

I jumped. The voice that spoke was low, rich, adding an ember of seduction to the peace and tranquility. I followed it to the end of the bed where Allistair sat watching me in the silence. My hand dropped to my lap and I pushed the crimson sheets away, trying to ignore the soft texture between my fingers and the way it brushed my thighs.

My bare thighs.

I blinked.

"Where did my jeans go?" My throat was dry as the Sahara and my words came out in a rasp. I swallowed hard, over the thickness that was building. It was suffocating, and in the sweltering heat that continued to plague me, downright delirious.

"You burned them," he replied. That voice sent a shiver down my spine. "Moira dressed you while you slept. She thought you might feel most at home in... minimal clothing." His eyes roved over the pale flesh of my legs, past the plain black boyshort underwear, and up my very fitted shirt. My arms broke out in goosebumps and I clasped them across my chest, hoping he couldn't see my taut nipples through the thin material.

The predatory flash of his eyes and upturn of his lips said it all.

"Where is Moira? And why are you here? I thought you were dealing with—"

"Moira is out. Pestilence took her down to Bourbon Street to try and enjoy herself. We told her if your familiar is stressed, it will make the transition harder. I thought you would appreciate the small lie so that she would not be here feeling all of what happens next." He took a deep breath and stood to remove his suit jacket. "As for me, I would think that's quite obvious. You can't last more than a few moments without trying to feed and

I am the only incubus among us. We are going to...rectify this situation."

What the actual fuck?

I jumped up from the bed, but my legs got tangled in the sheets. I slipped on the cool stone floor, only catching myself *after* I landed on my ass. Legs splayed and arms bracing me, my position was utterly compromising from where Allistair stood. I jerked my head, flicking my long blue locks out of the way so I could glare at him properly.

"Rectify? You're not rectifying shit, asshole," I snapped, trying to crawl backwards, away from his probing gaze. Well over six feet tall and standing not five feet away, he could have ogled my breasts that were spilling out of my low cut tank top, but he didn't.

He kept those golden eyes on mine and lifted one eyebrow in question.

"We're back to this?" he asked lightly. Indignation swept through, but I didn't respond. Too scared of the words that might come out. "I see," he murmured lightly as he undid his cuffs links. "Well, why don't you tell me what you want?" he continued conversationally as he began to unbutton his shirt.

I swallowed hard, but the words didn't come.

Need and want were beating at me like a fucking battering ram, but I didn't want to give in. Not like this. Not when he—

"You knocked me out," I breathed, my anger and need going head-to-head.

What was wrong with me?

"I did what I had to," he said matter-of-factly. "War had this room specially prepared for your transition, and with you coming into it so quickly, we thought it best to move you early. Try to take the bite off before things get underway."

I grit my teeth, snapping my legs shut as I moved to stand. Of course Allistair was there. Offering his hand like the perfect gentlemen. I slapped him away, grimacing when he stumbled back several feet.

Fucking strength.

Fucking transition.

Fucking Horsemen thinking they could decide what's best for me.

And Moira? Had she really gone along with this?

Sweat trickled down my back as the fever climbed to all new heights. I was going to die from dehydration before anyone stuck their dick anywhere.

"Ruby, I know that it's difficult for you to be rational right now, but I need you to trust me," Allistair crooned. It took him no time at all to recover and approach me again, using his lovely voice in an attempt to subdue me.

Bastard thought pretty words would fix it? Think again.

He wasn't the first of our kind I'd had to deal with.

"Trust you?" I breathed harshly. "You knocked me out against my will and brought me devil knows where"—I waved my hand around the room, only then noticing the assortment of *instruments* on the far wall—"without my permission. I don't have to do anything motherfucki—"

"Let me take the edge off so we can discuss this some-what rationally," Allistair interrupted. The button-up shirt he wore slipped from his shoulders, falling to the

24

ground haphazardly. It probably cost more than my mortgage, but he didn't give a damn. His gaze remained on me as he padded forward, barefoot and now shirtless, wearing only black slacks and cool arrogance.

I glowered at him and turned to look for a door in far corner of the room, making every attempt to step around Allistair. He grabbed my hand before I could make it two feet, snapping me back to him like a ball attached to a string. I hit his chest with a thump.

Anger. Desire. Betrayal. Want. Fear. Need.

They swirled together like the winds of an incoming storm. My desperation heightened as the beast inside me thrashed with rage. I didn't understand what was going on. I couldn't process it.

Couldn't process anything.

Moira had left me with them to—to—fuck them.

Brand them.

Submit to them.

Transition with them.

I couldn't understand it. Wouldn't understand it.

They had not earned the right to be the demons that brought me over. In fact, they had taken that choice from me. Assuming they could push the issue. Push me.

"I have no desire to push you or take your choice away, Ruby, but if someone doesn't take the edge off, you will hit the transition in a very bad place, even more confused than you are now. If that is what you wish, then I will take a seat right over there." He motioned to a large overstuffed armchair on the other side of the room. Beside it was a rack of restraining equipment. Collars, leather and metal bindings, varying lengths of leash with clips on the end—all hung from the pegs on the wall. "And I will remain until you tell me otherwise. However, I don't think that's what you really want."

Once again, my insides liquefied just being in close proximity to him. This back and forth within was giving me whiplash, making me all the more desperate to find my way back to sanity. If only the burning would cease...

Long elegant fingers trailed up and down my sides in a motion that should have been soothing, but wasn't. My skin had become hypersensitive in the time I slept. His fingers would have only been the barest of a brush before, but now funneled fire and heat into my veins and through every essence of my being.

"Will it stop?" I breathed, pressing my hands against the contoured planes of his chest. My breath was coming in short, fast bursts and he was barely touching me. Maybe this wasn't the worst idea...

"Stop? No," he replied, straight to the point. "Lessen? Yes. You should have a short reprieve where you can think about this with a clearer head." His heart shuddered beneath my palm, but the stroke of his thumb around the underside of my breast was steady.

Control. Allistair was very much in control.

Me? Not so much.

I slid my hands up his chest, running my fingertips along the edges of scars that had long since faded. A heady swelter built inside me, making my legs sway. I reached my hands around the back of his neck and gripped the firm muscle, digging my nails into despicably soft hair. Why couldn't it feel like a porcupine? That would make this so much easier. Of course the incubus had to have hair more luscious than mine.

"No sex. I'm clearly not thinking right." I gripped him tighter, but his head didn't move an inch. I guess that newfound strength was as unreliable as my fire. "You teach me to feed and that's it. You hear me?" My words would have sounded a lot bolder were I not panting from the feel of him pressed against me.

"I think you will find that feeding can be quite addictive," Allistair mused as he slipped his fingertips under my shirt, teasing the soft flesh. I gasped, and he chuckled.

Prick.

"Answer the question."

I wasn't willing to close my eyes and give myself into this without his word. Maybe I shouldn't be so trusting, given we were demons and all, but he was Famine. One of the Four Horsemen. There was no law I could hold him to, no promise I could make him keep. No matter how this went down, I had to trust that he meant what he said, because at the end of it, he was the only one that could hold himself to it.

"No sex *this time*. You have my word," Allistair replied. His lips twisted into an arrogant smirk as his hands continued their light ministrations. I groaned, both in frustration and desire. Satan damn him. He was going to be my undoing and we were barely even started.

You know what, though? Two could play at that.

I drew him in and Allistair leaned closer, allowing me better access as I brushed my lips across his jaw. His hands paused around my waist and I wriggled my hips a little, pushing my lower stomach against him. His erection twitched and the breath hissed between his lips.

"What are you doing, little succubus?" he breathed. I paused, noting the dangerously low tone of his voice. Like maybe I had pushed him too far, but the beast inside didn't think this was anywhere near far enough.

I moved my hands to either side of his shoulders and pushed.

His body yielded, stumbling back onto the bed and falling softly onto those blood red sheets. I didn't wait for his shock to wear off as I straddled his lap. The beast hummed a nod of approval as I wrapped my arms around him and ground my hips into the hard erection beneath me.

The fever-induced delirium blotted out all sense of rationality. I quickly forgot the point I was making and instead sought something infinitely more primal.

Release.

Allistair was the first to move, sweeping up to kiss me so hard our teeth clanked. A normal person might have stopped to think that this bestial urge came out of nowhere once again, but as his tongue parted the seam of my lips, all resistance flew out of my mind.

I groaned. This man kissed like a God. I always thought myself a good kisser, but Allistair wasn't like the sloppy boyfriends I'd had the last few years. He pried me apart with such expert precision I didn't realize I'd finally relaxed and was losing myself in him until I was already gone. Those skillfully long fingers wrapped around my wrists. He drew my arms behind my back where he switched his grip and held both wrists in one hand.

I struggled against him, testing my own strength. Once again, it was gone, leaving me a not very reluctant prisoner to an incubus with a free hand and many more lifetimes' worth of practice.

"Much better," he purred.

I shuddered at the way his voice floated over my skin. I'd underestimated him. He wasn't just some jo-schmo incubus off the street. He was pure seduction. Raw desire. His skin itself was a powerful enough aphrodisiac to make even the strongest woman lose her mind.

All this time I'd been worried about taking his choice away when he could have so easily taken mine. My body trembled with uncontrollable desire.

"What are you doing to me?" I muttered as his free hand slipped underneath the back of my thigh, pulling my arms tighter, my back arching as I was pulled up onto my knees. Fingers skated over my skin with feather light touches. He cupped my ass, squeezing it like he couldn't help himself as his hips rolled up, barely skimming me. My lips parted in a low moan as sensation wrapped around me, and I wouldn't let go.

Devil save me. I was going to need to feel a whole hell of a lot more to get my release, but at this rate I would be begging for him to just fucking do it.

"Allistair." I bit his bottom lip in warning and sucked. He tasted of blood and scotch, a spiced tang that could make me high. He groaned, and my traitorous body tried to inch closer even as he tightened his hold, eliminating any wiggle room I might have had.

"So savage, little succubus. Is it pain that you're craving?"

"Are you going to show me how to feed, or keep being a twatwaffle—"

His hand slipped between us and rubbed through the material of my boyshorts. My eyes rolled back in my head as my hips followed his command.

"I asked you a question, Ruby. No need to be rude."

His voice lulled me deeper into the desperate haze, my fever inching higher with every point of contact between us. The sound of him. The smell of him. The feel of him. All of it sent me spiraling into a version of me that I had never known. I was passion. I was desire. I was burning.

"I need an answer. Is it pain you are craving, or will you submit to me while I teach you how to feed?"

His torturous fingers slid further between my legs, hooking a single one through the thin strip of cotton. It brushed across my bare skin, feeling the dampness there as his did it.

"I submit to no one," I groaned.

"Ruby," he said in warning. "I'm losing my fucking mind right now wanting to be inside you. We both need to feed, and you asked me not to screw you six ways to Hell. Which means you have two options"—he paused to rub the back of his finger against my entrance and my hips gently swayed with him—"You either submit to me, or I bring Julian in here and you *will* submit to him. What's it going to be?"

The beast inside me wanted them all. At the same time.

She was a filthy slut that way.

I wasn't sure I would survive them both at once. Let alone four.

But the thought did have its merits...

I groaned as Allistair rubbed back and forth, teasing.

"I don't need pain right now," I bit out. Allistair smirked, but he wasn't letting me off so easily.

"Then what will you do?" he asked softly.

We were back to this. Of course, we were fucking back to this.

"I'll..." He arched an eyebrow. Daring me to say it. It was almost enough to rile the beast, but that wasn't what I wanted right now. "I'll do as you *ask,*" I said eventually.

For a moment I thought he was going to keep pushing until he heard what he wanted, but even Allistair was not patient enough for that. He crooked his finger and tore the fabric of my panties straight down the middle in one swift motion.

"Very well," he said with a bite in his tone as he bared me to the air. "You are going to come. Hard. And when you do, I am going to feed on your sexual energy. It's going to feel like a tug, but do not worry. We've done this before."

Without warning, he plunged two fingers inside of me and I cried out in shock. He didn't miss a beat as he started pumping them in and out, slowly building a rhythm. My blood sizzled with the scorching desire that flooded me.

A thick cloud of smoke began to form around him, shimmering like molten gold. His thumb pressed against my clit and the smoke drifted outward, molding around us. Shaping us. It fanned my skin, making the hairs tingle with energy. I shuddered against his fingers and they didn't relent.

"More," I breathed as I tried to writhe on his lap, but Allistair didn't give an inch. My back arched with my arms securely behind me and his grip kept me pushed up onto my knees as I tried to take all that he would give. Allistair hummed in approval, leaning down to press his mouth to my right nipple.

"You know the rules."

Sucking it hard, he whorled his tongue around the peak, inching me higher and higher as his fingering slowed. His thumb made lazy circles around my sensitive nub, giving me enough pressure to drive me crazy, but never tip over the edge.

I growled at him and the bastard bit me. My aching core constricted, desperately reaching for my release, and I let out a groan in frustration that bordered on a cry.

"Say my name when you come."

Possessive bastard.

"Yes," he snapped. "I am."

I didn't even have time to reply before he left a trail of suckling kisses across my chest. He nipped at my other nipple and sucked it sharply, twisting his fingers simultaneously.

"Allistair!" I shouted. My body convulsed around him, tightening on his fingers where they still pushed greedily inside me as he took all of my pleasure and then some. Just when I thought the high would drop, there was that tug, suspending me in bliss. I ignited and the room itself shook with me.

All too soon the suspended orgasm ceased, leaving

me wiped and yet...as Allistair released my arms and allowed me to drop on his lap, the coarse material of his slacks rubbed me where his hard cock strained beneath it. I pushed into him, enjoying the deep groan that I didn't so much as hear, but felt.

He wanted me. *So why was he denying himself?*

Allistair reached down and grasped me by the hips, lifting me off him with ease and leaning over to place me on the floor in front of him.

"What are you—"

"Get on your knees." I blinked at the tone in his voice. It was deeper than usual. Huskier. Almost more...*desperate.*

I sat back on the cold floor, in-between his spread legs.

My heart hammered against my chest as I stared up at him from below. I'd never considered myself submissive in any way, but this side of him intrigued me. The side where I could almost feel him coming...unhinged. He wore his arrogance with a swagger that few could manage, but beneath it I sensed a desperation. His control was more for himself than for me.

"Will this do?" I asked softly.

"Yes."

I wanted to shudder as the gold dust around us pressed against my skin, tingling everywhere it touched. I swiped my tongue out over my bottom lip, tasting his blood mixed with something potent. Something...delicious.

"What you are tasting is called kama. It's the sexual energy that feeds our kind." His words hazily made their way into my brain as the curling gold particles pulled me to him. Urging me to come closer. Take more.

"Kama..." I muttered. "Like Kama Sutra?"

Allistair chuckled. "The very same."

I lifted a hand toward him, letting it hover only inches away. The shiny yellow substance coated my fingers and brought them to my face to examine. It really did look like gold dust. Tentatively, I raised my forefinger to my lips and licked the gold powder off. An insatiable urge hit me and I wrapped my lips around that finger, groaning deeply while I sucked it dry.

"Enough," Allistair snapped, drawing my attention back to him. I stared up, biting my forefinger softly. His pupils dilated and a low growl started in his chest. "It's not polite to toy with others of your kind, little succubus."

There was that edge to his voice that I remembered. The crisp cut of words sharp enough to sting flesh, but made a girl crave more.

"You're the one that keeps turning me down, Famine."

It wasn't entirely me that let that slip out. The beast was very, very close to the surface and through his own need I wasn't sure Allistair saw it. His nostrils flared and his pupils continued to grow. Darker. Fuller. Until there was not a speck of white in his eyes. He looked at me like every bit the Horseman he was. A monster to both worlds.

But so was I, and he did not scare us.

"Unbutton my slacks."

I stared, slack-jawed for a minute at the forwardness of his request. Wasn't I the one that had been goading this for weeks? Playing with him. Taunting him. I laid the law for no sex, but I needed to feed and he needed to fuck. That much was clear.

If me sucking my finger made him almost come unhinged...the beast pushed forward and blotted out the last of my hesitations.

I reached out, placing both my hands on his inner thighs, gripping him so I could shuffle forward. He groaned as my hands swept up, running over the tight muscles of his legs, slowly inching towards the hard bulge in his pants. He twitched when my palm slipped over him and I rubbed his hard length up and down twice.

"Unbutton my slacks," he repeated.

I pinched the zipper between two fingers and dragged it down with exaggerated slowness. Normally, I would have a snappy reply in hand, but it wasn't so easy when I was breathing in all this gold dust. His...kama. The damn dust made my brain go foggy, making it harder to hold onto thoughts and words when all I wanted to do was screw him. We even had a bed and everything...nope. Nope. I shook my head.

Suck. Not fuck. Got it, Ruby?

When the zipper was halfway down, I paused, and my lips parted as his erection forced it down the rest of the way.

"Commando?" I asked, my voice wasn't as light as I would have liked it to be. There was too much tension. Too much emotion swirling in my chest. Too much aching between my own legs.

Too much of the beast coming out.

Still, he didn't acknowledge it.

"I like to be prepared," he shrugged, but when I trailed a single finger along his length, I didn't miss the way his body tensed beneath me. I leaned forward, using my tongue to follow the same path as my finger.

He shuddered, and a single glistening drop formed on his tip. I was going to enjoy this very much.

I closed my lips around his swollen head, tasting his saltiness, careful to keep my teeth sheathed. Allistair groaned encouragingly and I took him in. His tip touched the back of my throat, making me gag once, coating my mouth in saliva.

He wrapped a hand around my hair and guided me forward. I went down, taking him deeper.

"Fucking hell, woman—you're going to kill me," he growled.

Allistair was not small by any means, but fuck, if he was any bigger I couldn't take him to the base. As it was, my eyes stung as tears began to form, but this power over him...this sense of what I could do to him—take from him —even while being at his mercy...

It was thrilling. Exhilarating.

It was...I breathed in through my nose and was unprepared for the sudden assault on my senses. I could only describe it as the most sensational experience of my life, where I existed everywhere and nowhere simultaneously. My body tingled with power, energy, kama—I pulled back, letting my tongue sweep across his underside and whorl around the tip. Allistair twitched in my mouth, and to my shock, the aching spot between my thighs throbbed hard.

I lifted my gaze to him, eyes flashing with accusation.

While it was my mouth he was taking, his kama made it feel like more. A small smile played on his lips as he watched me.

"Feels much better than you thought it would, doesn't it?"

My only response was dropping my left hand as I began rubbing myself.

"When I come, my kama will start pouring out. You're going to need to breathe it in, Ruby. Envision yourself pulling as much as you can inside you," he said through gritted teeth. I sure as hell didn't need the encouragement. This was fucking great.

The beast thought so too, but I was so far gone I didn't notice.

I sucked hard on him, whirling my tongue over the tip one last time before Allistair gripped my hair tighter. As he guided me down, he thrust up once, forcing me back to his base in one go. My eyes burned with tears and my core felt hotter than the flames of Hell as he thrust himself down my throat. I rubbed myself in fevered circles, rapidly approaching my own climax with him.

Oh fuck yes.

I moaned around him, swallowing once more and he came undone. His come hit the back of my throat as he took several shallow thrusts, and then...*kama.*

As he said, it poured out of him and into me. Seemingly knowing what to do, I breathed in, trying to focus on that as I brushed over my clit and came apart. My fingers went lower, dipping two inside of me, riding out my own climax while taking as much as I could from him.

Spots burst behind my eyes, bright flashes of white

against the blackness that took me for a few seconds. When my vision slowly came back, and my body stopped throbbing, I realized I still had my lips wrapped around Allistair and he had yet to *let* me move.

I started to pull away but had two palms flat against both sides of my head. Holding me there.

Control freak.

"*Mine,*" a presence growled back.

The possessiveness of it pushed at the beast's control and she snapped. High on kama and brimming with power, she shot forward. In the mere blink of an eye, she took all control and laid her hand flat against his lower abdomen. Allistair moved to readjust, but she gripped the base of him with the other hand, swallowing around the half-hardened cock in her mouth as it twitched. Allistair dug his hands into her hair, but I don't think he realized which Ruby he was playing with, not until she pulled on the tiniest seed of flame and poured in on his stomach. The burning slowly started to build. Certainly long enough he should have known what was going on, but he didn't stop it.

Why didn't he stop it?

Panic started to build within me, but the beast kept a firm claim on control. I'd made it perfectly clear in her mind that he was an acceptable mate. We were both on the same page, which meant he was hers to claim.

Allistair had to have known this. Had to have somehow realized, and yet his dick hardened, and he held both sides of my face with a fervor. The beast looked up at him with coy eyes, and there was no doubt in my mind. He knew, and he arched into her touch.

The burning in her palm intensified as the magic hit a boiling point. The breath hissed between his teeth as she branded our mark onto him. He let out a harsh groan, pulling her in...pulling her closer...

She pulled back. Her right hand curled where she was branding him, and her left stroked him with powerful thrusts. I would have been scared shitless that I'd accidentally rip his dick off with the strength running in my veins, but the beast wasn't worried. She used her considerable strength to bring him right to the brink of climax again. Her tongue licked at his head, but just before he could thrust up, she released him and leaned away.

Allistair reached for her, not giving a damn about the blazing blue pentagram that shifted on the "V" of his hips.

He slid one hand into the curve of my neck to guide my jaw, wrapping the other roughly in my hair. I would have let this go on. I knew that in my heart of hearts. I would have sucked him off again, and quite possibly let him take it further.

I would have let him shatter me, as I very well suspected he would have—promises be damned—had a door not just been thrown open.

I blinked and Allistair paused for a fraction of a second. He didn't ease up on me, but he also didn't pull me closer.

"I felt the ward straining..." Julian's voice trailed off at the sight of me, basically nude, face flushed, and lips parted to take the erect cock not six inches from my face. "She's fed," Julian surmised. The raw cold that emanated from him sapped the heat right out of me, and with it the beast left too.

I pulled out of Allistair's grasp, my strength once again temporarily overriding his. My thighs slapped the smooth marble as I toppled sideways, coughing hoarsely. Allistair growled under his breath and Julian stayed at the entry point, arms crossed over his chest. Without a handle and only smooth cream paint, the doorway I hadn't previously realized was a doorway blended in with the rest of the wall. But clear as day, he stared at me with hard green eyes, unreadable if I were only looking at what my eyes saw. Desire and wariness were the bulk of his feelings, outside the small spark of envy he was still trying to temper.

"See something you want?" I snapped at him, feeling insanely irritable over the jealousy that continued to eat at him. The jealousy that he was choosing to ignore like a fucking child and not a grown male. It just made this whole thing even more complicated and difficult for me to wrap my head around.

"What are you talking about?" he asked, but it wasn't in the flirtatious way Allistair liked to do things. Julian was honestly still trying to play this game. To act like if we both ignored it, that it would magically go away.

"Never mind," I coughed leaning back against the wall. Allistair at least had the decency to get up and fetch me a drink. Meanwhile, Julian stood there, his smoldering gaze eating through any and all pretenses of what was really going on here. I rolled my eyes and accepted the glass of amber liquid Allistair offered to me.

"Wha-what is th-this?" I choked out, tipping it back.

"Two-hundred-year old scotch."

I spluttered for a second and then swallowed it down before coughing even harder than I already was.

"What the actual hell? Why on earth do you think scotch is appropriate when someone's coughing—"

"Why would I not share my scotch with my *mate*?" There was a twinkle in his eye as he said it and it confirmed my suspicions. Allistair genuinely wanted to be claimed. Just as Laran had, and just as Rysten still wanted.

But Julian was another story.

He was willfully blind and the kind of jealousy he felt for them would only get worse if it continued. We were supposed to be together forever. Literally until the end of time because they were my protectors. At best, this was going to make our relationship difficult if he kept it up. The beast wanted him. She wanted all of them, but forever was a long fucking time to deal with this nonsense.

I averted my eyes from Allistair and said to no one in particular, "I want a bath. I want to see Moira. Then I want to talk. In that order."

Julian's jaw twitched, but otherwise he didn't let his annoyance show.

"Any other demands?" Allistair snapped, turning standoffish.

I knew it hurt his feelings on some level. That while he had wanted this—I hadn't seriously thought about it, but my wishy-washy attitude on the subject was a little too late now that the beast went and made another life changing decision. Julian's presence only served to

41

remind me I needed to think—because as soon as I entered the transition it was all over. That much I was painfully clear on.

"Yeah, actually"—I pointed to the half-full bottle of scotch Allistair was holding—"I want the rest of that. I think I'm going to need it."

ALLISTAIR

I could rip his dick off and shove it down his throat until he choked on it.

Unfortunately, Death could not die, and I had more class than that.

Watching Ruby flee from the room with my scotch in hand was one of the harder things I've had to endure. There were many types of bonds and brands, but the mating bond and branding was a special sort engagement. For me to be branded and claimed as the second mate was what I wanted, but for her to act that way after doing so...stung.

My fingertips traced the edges of the dark blue pentagram. Julian coughed from the doorway, his pointed way of saying to put a shirt on because he's a jealous bastard and can't handle it.

"Is there something you needed, Death? Or do you just enjoy being a masochist?" His glare turned brutal as winter in the Arctic circle.

"Don't fucking start with me, Famine."

I cocked an eyebrow. "Don't start with you? You interrupted us about *the wards*—that we both know would have held through the first feed." His eyes flashed, and he looked away. *Yeah, I'm aware of how well enforced they are.* "Admit it, Julian. You're being a bastard because you don't want to share, but you don't want to make a move."

"You don't know what you're talking about—"

"I can read your fucking emotions. Cut the shit. I know why you're here. Care to tell me how long you stood outside before interrupting?"

I adjusted my slacks despite the extremely uncomfortable case of blue balls I had thanks to the she-demon who ran out on me because of this prick. I'd never had a girl leave my bed before. Or one that could walk properly after we were done, for that matter. Then again, Julian had never dared cockblock me.

"Long enough," he replied.

His way of saying he never left. Some would have been enraged by that, perhaps Julian himself, given the shame he felt, but I couldn't afford that luxury. Not when we all had too much riding on us—Ruby especially—to let their unresolved issues fester into a hard resentment.

As much as it pained me to cover her brand, this was not a normal engagement and would require more tact than any of them had. I found the dress shirt I'd discarded on the floor and put it back on, being sure to button it up properly and put on my cuff links before I turned back to him.

"Did you hear my offer to her when she started to

44

resist?" I asked him. Again, he gave a non-committal mutter under his breath. I took that as a yes. "Because if you did," I paused, "you should know that the possibility...intrigues her."

Julian tensed, and it was that stillness of a predator, even more lethal than I, that told me how affected he was by her.

"I don't share," he said eventually. I shook my head as he turned to leave.

"You don't get a choice."

Julian rounded on me. "You know why I'm staying away. Why I *have* to stay away."

I did, but I didn't think his reasons were good enough. Much as I would have liked to keep her for myself, I could share if it meant keeping some part of her. I could let her be a Queen with four consorts, so long as it was only us.

But Julian couldn't.

"There are bigger monsters than you in this world now, and one of them has chosen you as its mate. You cannot walk away because of duty, and yet you won't give her what she wants. You think you can't share?" I let out a dark chuckle and his eyes flashed in warning. "Imagine the next eternity of watching this while you play the sad, pathetic time of her transition over and over again in your head, asking yourself why you made the most idiotic decision of your existence." I paused when his head bobbed and fists clenched. If he was this close to losing it, then her transition should go about as well as the beast's tantrums. "I cannot make a decision for you, and frankly I don't know why I'm forcing this conversation when less of you means more time with her for me. You need to get your head out of your ass where she is concerned. You will never have any part of her and will ruin any feelings she may hold for you if you keep acting like an adolescent boy and continue to run away from the reality of our situation. Mate with her or don't, but don't make her feel like shit in the meantime. She has too much on her plate already to deal with your self-pitying attitude."

There had only been a hand full of times in our existence that I had to save Julian from himself. As I walked through the mirror and left him to think alone, I wondered if I would look back one day and realize this was one of times. If me pushing him would be the thing he needed to finally work past his own demons, or if the very thoughts themselves would be too much for him to handle and would ultimately consume him.

CHAPTER 4

Julian may have rolled his eyes, but I got the rest of the scotch.

Half an hour later, sitting in the Jacuzzi tub, I couldn't be bothered to give a shit about much of anything as I drained the last bit of the bottle and set it aside. The jets worked away at the tension in my shoulders, and for the first time in the last sixteen hours I felt like some semblance of my usual self. A pounding head from interesting life choices and drinking a crap ton of booze beat out lighting shit on fire and throwing myself at the Horsemen any day.

There was a knock at the door before it swung open.

"You know, you can't keep hiding out in here forever."

Moira's voice drifted over me as she walked into the bathroom, barefoot but dressed like she just got back from clubbing. She wore a little black dress and onyx stud earrings that reflected in the dim light. Her dark green hair was pulled back into a massive ballerina bun, not a single hair out of place. It made her blue eyes pop and the pentagrams swirled. The devil's mark—my mark—forever branded on her.

"I'm not hiding," I lied. "I just don't feel well."

Moira gave me a no-nonsense kind of look and I groaned leaning back to rest my head on Bandit since he chose to sprawl out on the edge of the bathtub behind me. He purred, curling his tail around my neck. I absent-mindedly reached back to scratch him behind the ear.

"Of course you don't feel well. You're entering the transition. I'd be shocked if you did." She came to sit behind me, her footsteps almost silent against the stone floor. "Every time you're around one of them, you either want to fuck 'em or kill 'em, and funny as it is...that's not you. It's the hormones, or whatever you want to call it." I felt her hands in my hair as she undid the messy knot I'd pulled it in and began working through the tangles.

"I'm frustrated they feel they can tell me what to do and decide what's best for me, and given the complicated relationships at the moment, I don't think that's unrea-sonable," I grumbled. Moira gently massaged my scalp, her steady warmth and contentment bleeding into me.

"They are...trying. This isn't exactly the most conven-tional situation. You're a hell of a lot more powerful than they expected, and your moods are all over the place. Sorry, but it's true," she added when I opened my mouth to object. "Plus, the beast has already made it clear she intends to claim them. Not to mention the whole familiar thing, which we haven't even gotten a chance to talk about." I opened my mouth to apologize and she tugged a little on my hair. "Don't even think about apologizing. There's enough crap going on. It can wait until we have a chance to breathe. Seriously. I've been your familiar for years if the Horsemen are right. You branding me just makes it official."

I don't know how I ended up so lucky to have a best friend like her. For as crazy as she may be, she was the rock I needed when the world went to shit. A tear pricked my left eye, and I wiped it away before it had the chance to fall.

"Are you upset that I branded you?" I asked quietly, increasingly aware of the sound of water dripping from the faucet and three heartbeats filling the huge space.

"Hell no. Why on earth would you think that?" She didn't even have to think about her answer.

"Because I know how you feel about branding in general and I don't want you to think this means I own you or some shit. I'm not that kind of demon." I swallowed hard. "I didn't mean to...I just wanted to save you." Moira released my hair and came around to sit on the side of the tub.

"You don't need to apologize for this, Ruby," she said and motioned to her eyes. "I know what kind of demon you are, and I know you didn't brand me out of some fucked up possessive complex. You saved my life, and the way I see it is Hell is going to be a lot safer with your mark on me. No one fucks with a demon carrying the devil's pentagram. People will think twice before trying something." I reached over and took her hand, squeezing it gently. She wrapped both of hers around mine and squeezed back. "The Horsemen are also fucking livid

49

because they were supposed to be your familiars. I like that being one means they can't just take you from me. They and everyone else knows where the score is now."

I chuckled under my breath. Of course she would see it that way.

"We're a package deal," I agreed.

"Yup. You, me, and the trash panda," Moira snickered. Bandit grumbled and tucked his tail tighter around me.

"Raccoon," I corrected her.

"He *literally* ate trash before you took him in. You can't even argue he's like a less domesticated cat. He ate trash—"

Another knock at the door and it cracked open.

"Everything okay in here, love?" Rysten called.

"We'll be out in a minute," I said. Moira rolled her eyes as the door slammed shut. "How was Bourbon Street with him?"

She groaned. "It's hard to have fun when you're being babysat by someone who doesn't want to be there. I swear, he spent the whole time pouting because you were back here, and he didn't want to be on 'Moira duty'. What the fuck is that anyways?"

"Well, I'm sorry you couldn't get laid," I chuckled, not feeling all that sorry. I'm sure she'd have a plethora of demons lining up at her door in Hell, where I hoped she would be safer.

"Speaking of getting laid"—she paused and raised an eyebrow—"what's the deal? I could tell you were having some *issues* earlier. Is it the whole branding thing? What's going on there?"

Oh man.

I wasn't sure I wanted to have this conversation, but I was running out of time where choice would even be an option. Pulling my head up from Bandit, I slowly scooted forward so I could get out of the tub. The warm air fanned my wet skin, making my head feel fuzzy.

"It's complicated. I do want them. All of them, but we've got some issues to sort out. I don't want them making choices for me."

That was putting it mildly. We had several big problems to sort through, but I wasn't sure how much I felt like going through it all in my very limited time with Moira. I released her hand to step out of the tub and my toes curled into the shaggy white rug beneath me.

"Me being pissed with Allistair when I woke up could have been avoided if they'd told me, 'hey, you need to feed' versus knocking me out and putting me in a room with him. That really wasn't cool, and while I do feel better, that doesn't excuse that it was a shitty thing to do." I reached over for a fluffy white towel and dried myself off.

"I don't know if you can tell, but to the rest of us you haven't been thinking that clearly. You gotta remember that, and this is coming from me. You know I'd shove my foot up any of their asses if I thought they were doing something they shouldn't be, but as it is, you started a fire in the living room. A fire no one but you can control." She paused to press her lips together in a troubled smile. "I didn't think what Allistair did was all that smart. I told them it would probably piss you off more, but I also get why they did it... the bigger thing here is I'm trying to make sure this is what you want, because you already claimed that fuckface, War, and pretty boy, Famine. Pest is champing at the bit to be next. So if you don't want this..."

She left her prompt in the air, but we both knew what she meant. If I don't want this, it's a little fucking late. Brands can't be undone.

Wish someone would have gone and told the beast that before she pulled this.

I shook my head turning to the opaque white counter where a pair of yoga pants and my favorite tank top undershirt sat waiting for me. In Oregon, it had been too cold to wear anything sleeveless this time of year, but down in New Orleans and its sticky Louisiana heat, the humidity stayed year-round.

I dressed slowly, taking my sweet time while I tried to sort through my thoughts. Already the fuzziness was starting up again. I didn't give myself an hour before I was delirious.

"My life was already changing faster than I was comfortable with. Now I'm starting the transition to becoming immortal with two mates, but the beast wants more." I pressed my hands together, twisting my fingers around. "It's not the sex that gets me here. It's my lack of control in branding them. I didn't mean to brand Laran. I sure as fuck wasn't planning on branding Allistair. The beast did that shit, and now they're both my mates even though we haven't consummated it. She wants all of them and I have no way of stopping myself from tying them to me in every way." I paused, finally feeling like I was getting to the crux of the matter. "But what if they don't want that? I mean—I *know* Rysten does, but Julian? He's made it pretty clear he doesn't want to go further, even though he's greener than you. He should get the right to choose that, just like Allistair and Laran should have... but I'm afraid if they don't want me, the beast isn't going to let *any* of them choose someone else either..."

I let out a heavy sigh, my shoulders folding in. I cared about the guys. All of them. I really did, but would I feel that way in hundred years? What about a thousand? I already had Laran and Allistair to worry about. Having this talk with them wasn't going to be nearly as easy as it was with Moira. Having it with all four of them? The idea of it made my head spin.

I leaned my hip against the counter and rubbed my temples. I guess this is what it means to have demon problems and commitment issues, but what could you expect out of someone who couldn't give a guy a blowjob without them going nuts?

"Okay, first, Julian is fighting a losing battle. We all know this. Hell, even the trash panda knows it—" She broke off to frown as Bandit let a chittering kind of...*laugh*. Almost like he was chuckling. "Point is, he'll get over it. Second, have you met the four of them? Are we talking about the same Horsemen?" Moira asked, crossing her arms over her chest. I scrunched my eyebrows together, confused as to where she was going. "Because those four have been fucking crazy about you ever since they showed up."

"That doesn't mean they wanted to spend forever with me, Moira." Bandit walked over and tugged on my pants, signaling for me to pick him up. "Or that I wanted

53

to spend forever with them," I added as I gathered him in my arms.

"You're spending forever with them whether you fuck them or not," she pointed out, tapping her foot almost impatiently.

"Yeah, and I'd rather the beast not try to rip anyone's balls off because they decided they didn't want to be with me anymore, or with me to begin with," I snapped, impatient as hell back. Her own moodiness at my hesitation was bleeding over into me.

"But if you can't stop it, then it's going to happen either way." She lifted both eyebrows and pursed her lips, making her point. "And have you stopped to even ask them how they feel instead of just assuming? I mean, for devil's sake, Ruby, their entire existence is wrapped around you. In their eyes you could have hung the fucking moon, babe."

"Didn't we already have this talk about diving into things without about thinking it?" I asked in almost whine. Bandit held onto me tighter and used one paw to stroke my cheek. Moira rolled her eyes.

"Yes. We did, and we came to the conclusion that you're the fucking Queen of Hell whether you like it or not. This is no different, Ruby." She marched right up to me and grabbed me by my chin, pulling me down to her level. "You've got four insanely hot guys that that beast of yours chose and sitting here in denial isn't going to change that," she said in a calming voice. "Now you can she-demon up just like you've done with everything else in your life, or you can sit in here being pouty and drinking scotch. What's it going to be?"

My lips pressed together as I glanced over at the empty bottle.

I knew this. I knew before we even talked what I needed to do. I just didn't want to admit it.

But that's the thing: I either keep up with the program, or one of these times the problem will get ahead of me. I wasn't going to let that happen.

I was Ruby Morningstar, for devil's sake.

I'd found out I was Lucifer's daughter and survived multiple assassination attempts. I'd lived through abuse and came out stronger. I'd learned I had more gifts than I ever thought possible, and now—I was going to transition like a motherfucking boss.

Hopefully. Because it's not like this job came with a training manual.

And I was running out of options.

CHAPTER 5

The sun was peeking over the horizon when I stepped into the living room. An inch-thick glass wall was all that separated me from the wonders and dangers of New Orleans. Out there, somewhere, was the portal to Hell, but at the moment I had greater things to worry about. They came in the form of four dangerously seductive demons, who all happened to be waiting for me.

"You seem to be feeling better," Allistair smirked from across the room. He sat shirtless, leaving the blue brand across his abdomen on display. His arm sprawled across the back of the long leather couch where a vacant seat was waiting between him and Rysten.

Damn him. He was no better than Laran. They both got far too much enjoyment out of this for the wrong reasons. On one hand, it made me want to throttle them. On the other...maybe Julian could use the prodding to make him sort through his shit...

"I am, thanks for asking," I said, displaying a smirk of

my own and crossing my arms over my chest. Instead of taking the waiting seat between them, or the one beside Laran, I veered straight for the single armchair. Bandit leapt on top of it, poising himself where he could simultaneously watch them and be petted.

"We need to discuss your transition," Julian said, turning away from the cityscape. "Or more pertinently, how you would like to go about it." Both his arms were clasped behind his back. He wore dark pants and a fitted long sleeve shirt, despite the New Orleans heat—then again, maybe it was just me burning up given how high the air conditioner was jacked. His jaw tensed, waiting for my answer. The picture of utter control.

"Ummm..." I drawled out. "I don't know. Considering no one ever thought I would transition, I didn't pay all that much attention to the house mothers at the orphanage..." My voice trailed off at the look he and Rysten were sharing. Allistair sighed deeply, and even Laran looked a bit uncomfortable.

"You have no idea what the transition entails?" Julian asked slowly.

I shook my head. "Not really. Theoretically, I know that I might gain some cool powers and I'll stop aging, as for how..." I shrugged. "Like I said, I never thought I would."

The room seemed to let out an audible sigh of frustration. Clearly the Horsemen had expected more than that. Expected more of me. It's not like I signed up for this job, though. I had no idea until they showed up on my doorstep to drop the news. The awkward silence made me tense and I looked away as Moira came to sit on the other arm of my wide chair, throwing her arm around me. She smelled a bit like sweat and booze. Great.

"It might be a bit easier, love, if we started with your questions and worked from there," Rysten suggested. His lips quirked up in an encouraging smile.

"Well..." I started when Moira decided to cut in.

"Let's start with you Four Hobos."

Did she really just call them that? Yep. Yes, she did.

"Her beast wants to claim all of you. Is there going to be any issues here? Because she's all caught up on not wanting to take anyone's choice away—"

"I think that's enough, Moira," I cut in. My eyes narrowed at her as she shrugged her slim shoulders.

"I'm tired. It's six in the fricken' morning and we're holding an intervention. Someone had to break the ice."

And you clearly appointed yourself in charge of that.

I think I went indigo from head to toe with the way the four of them were watching me. I moved my hands to my lap and twiddled my thumbs; behind me, Moira let out a groan.

"Is that what she really thinks?"

The words drifted through my mind. Sudden and without preamble.

Where had that come from?

I frowned.

"I would have branded her an hour ago if she was concerned where I stood."

Okay. I *know* that wasn't me. Something weird was going on here.

"Ruby, love, you are aware that harems are quite

common in Hell, aren't you?" Rysten asked, the first to break the silence as far as I could tell.

"Yeah," I said. "But you guys aren't normal demons. It's not unreasonable to think that each of you might want your own harems one day..." I trailed off, feeling sheepish under the look Laran was giving me.

"She really doesn't see herself the way we do."

I perked my head up, trying to figure out where the voice came from, but no one spoke. This was getting kind of awkward...

"Being chosen by the beast is the greatest honor we could receive—" Rysten started kindly.

"I don't give a damn about honor, Rysten. I need to know what you guys want. Each of you." I swallowed hard and looked at each of their faces. Julian: stoic. Rysten: thoughtful. Allistair: flirtatiously seductive. Laran: intense, as always. He sat shirtless, twin pentagrams already branded on his shoulders.

"I'm sorry I branded you. Both of you"—I cut my eyes between him and Allistair—"without talking first. I never would have—"

Laran moved, rising to his feet. The low-slung jeans on his hips did naughty things to me, but it was his imposing stare that kept me transfixed as he crossed the living room. He came to kneel before me and rested his large hands over mine. Bandit inched forward, rubbing himself against Laran and let out a purr.

"Never apologize for branding me. I would not have it any other way. You are my mate, Ruby Morningstar. Now and forever." The sincerity of his words made my blood rush. A slow, steady tempo building in my head. My heart. My body. It thrummed with power. *Heat.*

"Laying it on a little thick there, War?" another voice whispered unceremoniously.

Laran's teeth clenched oh so slightly, but they did. Could he hear it too?

"Ruby, you must understand that it is not our place, nor anyone's, to brand you first. Just as no other but you would be able to brand us. That is how things work in our world," Allistair inserted, lazily watching the scene between me and Laran.

His feelings felt different, though. While not jealous, he was...possessive. Not so dark or dangerous as the way I felt it from Julian, but I got the distinct impression he wanted to be doing very bad things with me right now. Maybe it was better he wasn't on his knees expressing his undying devotion like Laran.

"You are Lucifer's daughter. For us to claim you before you and the beast choose us...it would be presumptuous, at best, and a deadly insult, at worst. Think about what the beast would do if another male were to claim you now. Would she allow it?" he asked me already knowing the answer.

Outside of them? No. No, neither of us would. I shook my head.

"Precisely," he sighed. "We have not claimed you because we're waiting to be chosen. Not because we want a harem of our own. I think I speak for us *all* when I say that," Allistair continued pointedly. I didn't miss the sly glance he shot at Julian whose true emotions were hidden behind an impenetrable mask.

"You already know how I feel, love. If not for it being your first feed, I would have gladly taken Allistair's place," Rysten added.

The warm fuzzy feeling in me spread. The beast appreciated their devotion, but she was still a bit irked by Julian's lack of response. The way she saw it, she chose him, and he was pushing against her dominance as a mate. I wish I could back away slowly with both hands raised, but that's not exactly possible when two beings occupied one body.

"Her first feed?" Moira interrupted, pulling me back from the perilously close edge I hadn't realized I'd approached. The beast was trying to lure me back so she could come forward again.

"The first time a succubus or incubus feed, we need more kama," Allistair explained. "Our own kind produces more than another demon, and demons produce more than humans. Ruby could have fed from one of them the first time, but they would have been severely depleted." He cocked an eyebrow at me, and I pursed my lips. Was that admiration on his face? Pride?

"Or died. Given how she fed she may have actually killed one of them, but fuck that would have been some way to die. Her mouth wrapped around my cock was—"

Two fingers grasped my chin, pulling me forward. I turned my head and met Laran's insistent stare.

"We were created to be your equals. For us, that meant that no other female would be ours. Even if you did not claim us, we would never have our own harems. That's not how we were made," he said in complete and utter seriousness. That was War for you. Not a man of many words, but the few he said were profound. At least to me.

"That doesn't mean you *have* to choose this...or that all of you want it," I finished, turning my eyes to the only one who had yet to speak. The one I currently couldn't read. The real core of this problem. "Do you?"

Julian stared at me with the most beautiful eyes I'd ever seen. They were a shade of green so deep and vibrant that I could try for a hundred years and still wouldn't get the color just right. But for all their beauty, they were incredibly cold. Like death...

"I want to keep you safe," Julian said evenly.

"That's not what I asked."

His words were a chip to my heart, but I wouldn't show it. They gave me every other part of themselves freely. I would not demand this from them. From him. The beast be damned. I would not tie him to me if he didn't want that.

Even if the other three did. Even if this would cause issues for years to come.

For centuries. I still wouldn't do it.

I wouldn't take his choice away.

"He's a fucking idiot—"

"Can't he pull his head out of his ass for two fucking seconds—"

"He's not fooling any—"

I pulled away sharply, breaking Laran's grip on my chin to shake my head.

What was going on? No one's lips were moving. No one was speaking. Was I going crazy?

Was I hearing voices?

"Ruby, babe..." Moira said, sliding away from the arm of the chair.

Panic flooded me at the loss of contact. I hadn't realized how much she was holding me together. How much her exhausted state of calm was keeping the burning at rest. My hand whipped out, faster than lightning. I wrapped my fingers around hers, pulling her to her knees before me with a flick of my wrist.

She hit the ground about as gracefully as could be expected, shoving Laran on her way down.

"What's up? Talk to me, Rubes," Moira murmured, raising a small green hand to my cheek. She hadn't called me that in years, and now three times in one day?

Embers flared inside of me. They drifted through my veins, catching fire where they went, and I was helpless against it. Hopeless to stop myself as power surged within me.

So far, every gift I had developed was deadly.

The flames of Hell.

Soul shredding.

Feeding.

What would be next? What personal hell would fate cook up to test me?

How much could I take before I broke apart at the seams?

How hot could I burn before the world caught fire with me?

I wasn't sure, but the sweltering fever that was coming on again didn't leave me all that confident.

"So...*hot*..." I breathed, the words shaking as I said them.

The room seemed to look almost...glassy? Like when you stood outside on a day that was hot as hell and stared into the distance. The way it almost smeared together as the sun cooked the very earth.

But we were inside. In December.

Which meant...

"Can you hear me, Ruby?" Moira asked, a tenor of worry in her voice.

I don't know when or how, but suddenly everyone was there. Allistair was at my left. Rysten at my right. Laran kneeled beside Moira, and Julian stood right in front, assessing the situation with a clinical gaze if I ever saw one.

"The transition is speeding up," he murmured.

"Do we move her—"

What's going on?

"She's heating the room, Julian—"

Where are these voices coming from?

"Something's coming—"

What's coming? Why isn't anyone answering me?

"She's starting to lose it—"

I clasped my hands over my ears and let out a choked cry.

"What is she doing?"

Can't they hear me?

"Do you think it's—"

"Stop!" I shouted. A wave of power flashed through the room and the glass warbled. Fire ignited at my fingertips where I held Moira's hand, but she held tight as it inched up my bare arms.

"Rubes, I need you to talk to me..." Moira trailed off

as I raised my head and pulled her to me. Acting without thinking, I did the only thing that felt right in that moment.

I kissed her.

Never in my life had I felt anything sexual toward Moira, and this was no different. But a sudden burning desire to lay one on her filled me with a compulsion I couldn't control. I coaxed her lips apart with ease and breathed, exhaling the swirling tempest out of my chest and into her. I didn't understand what was going on. Why the power within was trying to claw its way out of me into anything. Into her.

Her lips pressed closed with a finality and I pulled away.

What the—

Of course, that's when she screamed—and I don't just mean any normal banshee scream. This was the sound of raw, undiluted pain.

And the very foundation itself trembled.

"Moira!" I cried, reaching out to her again. I didn't understand what had possessed me to do that, but the moment our skin made contact, the screaming died instantly, like someone cut her vocal cords.

She collapsed inward, her dark green hair spilling across my lap. I brushed my hand over her, my fingers snagging on something warm.

"What the—" I broke off as I turned her head.

Two tiny flaming horns poked out of her head, black and blue swirls coming together and solidifying in seconds, like the flames had frozen and been given form.

They couldn't have been larger than two inches, but they were hard as stone and wicked sharp.

"Horns," Rysten whispered.

"And wings," Allistair added dryly.

I turned my gaze to the massive pair of flaming blue wings, slumped over like the girl whose back they were attached to. Veins of cobalt and indigo colored the strands of fire. Sections of dark flame moved through them, seemingly shifting and turning while still maintaining shape.

But her wings...they did not solidify.

They burned.

I reached out, brushing my hands over the hot strands, but felt no heat.

"How is this possible?" I whispered, fighting to regain control of the situation. Moira had wings—and horns—although the latter wasn't terribly surprising. I always knew she had them, but now the rest of the world could see it too.

"It's hard to say," Allistair murmured. "But if I had to guess, you might have inherited more abilities from Lola than we initially thought. Your mother could imbue objects with magic."

"Imbue with magic?" I asked, fighting the bristling that was running down my spine and the beast's cool gaze. That bitch knew what was going to happen to Moira. She knew, and she didn't give a damn.

If anything, she waited, sulking in the back of my mind until the pressure became too much. She allowed the power that had been lying dormant in me to unleash suddenly and violently, knowing how I would react because she knew me better than anyone. Even myself.

I wanted to hate her, but hating the entity that lives within me wouldn't help anyone. We're a package deal. Even if she branded all of them without asking, just to further her own selfish desires. Cunt.

"Imbuing is using your own power to alter something, or in your case, someone. Lola used to create weapons that could do things I have never seen. You pushed Moira through the entire transition in seconds. She won't be just a half-demon anymore..." I brushed my hand over her forehead, Allistair's voice falling short at what we saw.

"Is that what I think it is?" I didn't want to ask, but I had to. I was terrified at what it meant, because I'd only heard of a mark like this once.

"The horned helmet never lies," Julian replied.

A horned helmet with two black wings.

A brand. Moira had a brand.

But not just any brand.

"She's a legion," Rysten said in disbelief. "You've got to be kidding me."

Suddenly the beast's smugness made a lot more sense. We didn't just give her horns and wings of flame. We'd made her damn near untouchable, because a legion bore the mark of Cain.

Yet another thing that humans fudged across time. I guess that's what happens when immortal beings come to a mortal planet and conquer. Eve was sent here as punishment by her sister, Lilith and Lilith's lover, big daddy Lucifer. She had turned on them in the war between immortals at the dawn of time. The whys and hows have never been clear, partly because Eve started to lose her mind once on earth. She fucked anything and everything that could walk, sometimes killing the men in the process. Across all of that, she had only ever bore three sons. Seth, who disappeared and was never heard from again. Abel, who died. And Cain, who killed him.

The bible leaves out that Eve had commanded him to do it. She claimed to have had a vision of a horned helmet with black wings, and should one of her children offer up a worthy sacrifice, they would be gifted with this mark.

Only Cain was willing to listen and find out.

Since then, the mark had shown up again only a handful of times across history. It was legendary, because it was real. Cain had gone on to slay many demons. After impregnating as many women as possible, he ventured to Hell. He was the first and only Seelie to do so.

He also never came back out.

The mark of Cain appeared only in exceptional circumstances to those truly willing to do anything and everything for a goal. A purpose. Cain was the only Fae known to bear it, but there were whispers of children marked by blood or rune magic in an attempt to see if it held. If it could be recreated. It was said that any who bore this mark returned pain sevenfold.

I didn't know if that was true.

But what I did know was that for all intents and purposes, my best friend and familiar just got a hell of a lot harder to kill.

Unfortunately, I was the one that did this to her because whatever powers I had were running rampantly out of control. Judging by the Horsemen's pained expressions, they had already come to that conclusion.

"It was an accident."

I seemed to be saying that a lot nowadays. Despite having the Four Horsemen, Bandit, and Moira at my side —I couldn't seem to stay out of trouble. Or stop setting shit on fire.

And judging by the beast's shit-eating grin, she wasn't about to stop anytime soon.

On the contrary, she was just getting started.

CHAPTER 6

I asked to see Moira for the hundredth time.

For the hundredth time, they said no.

"She's fine, love. Let her sleep it off," Rysten said.

I grumbled in response, leaning against the bed and ignoring the wall of instruments that had been taunting me for the last twelve hours. Shortly after Moira collapsed, they moved me back to my warded room, no matter how many times I protested. Eventually, Julian ordered War to move me whether I liked it or not.

Laran threw me over his shoulder and dropped my ass on the bed and he and Rysten had been watching over me since.

What they didn't realize was that the beast was pissed with them for it.

And so very close to the surface.

Julian had riled our anger, and very soon he was going to pay the consequences for that.

"*Careful, Pestilence. She almost persuaded you that time.*"

Had I? I hadn't noticed?

It didn't take long being stuck in here with them to realize the voices I was hearing were not voices at all, but thoughts. Their thoughts.

"*She's growing stronger. This bloody room is hotter than the fourth providence.*"

So it wasn't just me. That's nice. If they wanted to be assholes and lock me in here, at least they were sweating it out too.

"*She has fire in her veins. I expected nothing less.*"

How was it that War's internal voice could make me shiver? My cheeks warmed and I turned away, but not fast enough.

"Something wrong, love?" Rysten asked. He stood by the door, trying his best to look at ease and not like a guard. He failed.

"Nothing, I just—"

"Ruby, you're a terrible liar."

Oh crap. I could come clean that I'd been hearing their thoughts, and let's be honest, they were bound to find out soon enough. But it was nice having insight into the things they wouldn't normally tell me. For all I knew they had a way to turn it off, and I'd rather hear them than sit in silence like they thought I had been doing.

"Um—well—you see—"

Rysten lifted his eyebrows, a grin forming on his lips. Still, I don't know what persuaded me to say what I did next.

"I have to take a shit."

I couldn't believe I had just said that.

Just when I was going to retract my statement, my beast mentally shoved hard, not vying for control, but throwing me off-kilter long enough that by the time I looked up, Rysten had a tinge of pink on his cheeks.

"Oh, I see..." he trailed off, looking to Laran for help.

War sat in the lone armchair on the other side of the room because he was trying to keep his hands off me. Apparently, I smelled good.

"Should I let her go to the bathroom?" Rysten asked silently.

"If she has to shit, then she has to shit," Laran shrugged.

"Maybe I should ask Julian..."

Really? Now that irked the hell out of me. He didn't know I didn't actually need the bathroom, but he was going to ask Julian if I could go?

I bent, clasping my stomach. My motions were more guided by the beast than I wanted to admit. "I really gotta go, Rysten," I groaned. His decision wavered. "Unless you want me to shit on the floor..."

Rysten stepped into a shadow and disappeared. The next moment the door cracked open and he waved me forward.

"For the record, love, that's disgusting. Next time just say you need to go."

Isn't that what I started with? May as well make use of the opportunity...

As soon as I crossed through the ward, I knew something was up, but it wasn't until I closed the bathroom door behind me that I knew what.

"I'm right outside the door if you need me," Rysten called. I loudly grunted my response as I placed my hands on the bathroom sink.

A shudder ran through me.

What was that?

I stilled, pressing a hand to my chest. Nothing.

I breathed a heavy sigh and moved to use the bathroom.

Instantly, my stomach twisted in hard knots as a second shudder ran through me. I cried out once, leaning against the counter for support.

I had never been one to suffer from extreme cramps. Even my time of month was mild compared to Moira. But this was something else. I'd never felt a pain that wrapped around your insides and pulled like it was trying to tear apart every muscle.

I gasped in mouthfuls of air, but the reprieve didn't last long. A splicing sensation ripped through me, running straight from the apex of my thighs to the brand on my chest. It left a searing pain trailed by pleasure as it rammed into my sternum.

The pentagram pulsed. Once. Twice. Like a tidal wave it gathered its strength, building deep inside me, pulling from every essence of my being.

Laran had said I had fire in my veins. He wasn't wrong.

Those very veins lit up beneath my skin, casting me in an eerie light blue inside the semi-dark bathroom. My brand pulsed faster beneath my shirt, the outline showing up through the thin cotton tank top. I brushed my fingers against the fabric where it connected with my skin, and the brand flashed brighter. It began spinning beneath my shirt and an awful gut-wrenching feeling filled me.

This was it.

My shirt caught fire, erupting in a brilliant blaze that disintegrated not even a moment later. Heat engulfed me as I stumbled back from the bathroom counter. Head pounding. Heart beating. My knees hit the floor with a bang as flashing lights danced before my eyes.

Black. White. *Blue*.

The flames of Hell.

Banging.

I could hear banging in the distance as the Horsemen called to me.

It was too late for that. Too late for me.

Wrapped in a cocoon of flame and fire and ash, my conscience wavered.

I could feel it, my power approaching this crest as the tidal wave within swept through me. It built so far, so fast, that when the beast took my hand, I was glad. She could control it. She could get us through this when I couldn't.

Because there was no way I could possibly control what was coming.

Moira was just the beginning, and there was a hell of a lot more inside me where that came from. I saw a vision: a flaming girl with a crown of charred bones, sitting above a blackened city.

The Horsemen thought they could control me. They thought they were ready for me.

They thought wrong.

This was a pivotal moment where I could decide what part of me took control in transition.

But we both knew who I would choose when it came down to it.

We both knew what was coming.

My beast and I stepped into the flames of my soul together. We felt the immense power that lay there.

Power beyond what this world knew.

It didn't belong here.

We didn't belong here.

And in that moment, the future of both worlds was hanging by a single thread.

Because when it snapped, I would never be the same again.

"I will do what must be done," she whispered to me.

I believed her.

Maybe that was my first mistake. Maybe the fire and the heat had really gotten to me.

Or maybe it was what needed to be done for me to survive.

For Hell to survive.

Either way I would never know, because I wrapped my arms around her and the thread ignited.

And then we fell.

Fell into the flaming pits of my own self, where I would rise again.

Not as the half-breed I always thought myself to be.

But as the queen I must become.

When my eyes opened, they were not blue, but black.

I had hit the transition.

The bathroom door blew open. With her head bowed she could not see who, but she knew. She always knew.

The beast was so much cleverer than they gave her credit for.

They thought her wild and savage, but they failed to see how much she loved her games.

She raised her head to the Four Horsemen. Her mates.

Though one of them had yet to see it.

No matter.

They stared at her with a challenge and she smiled wickedly.

It was time to play.

RYSTEN

Power erupted like a shock wave through the apartment. Dread didn't have time to fill me, because I knew. I knew what was coming.

My fists smashed against the door as I tried to break it down, to tear it off its hinges. Soon that banging was not just me, but Laran as well. A second wave swept through, stronger than the first, and then we heard the screaming.

The transition was not kind. It was not enjoyable. For something that was mortal to become immortal, your own body would turn on itself. Your mind would go mad.

Ruby talked about burning before, but for someone as strong as her? I don't know how she would overcome it. Power comes with a price, and for the strongest of us, we pay the most.

My transition had been unbearable. I'd rotted from the inside out so long that I grew to resent the power of Pestilence. Julian's transition had killed him. Except

Death can't die, and so he lived and died, again and again, until it passed.

But Ruby? She was more than death or destruction, and judging by her screams, she was burning.

"Open the door, love!" I called out.

It was hopeless. Somehow, some way, she had sealed the bathroom. Where my strength alone should have removed the door with one hit, it stayed firm, not a single mark made.

She had to have imbued the entire fucking bathroom so no one could enter.

I doubt she even realized it.

A third shockwave ripped through the building.

"The wards aren't going to hold her."

"There is a plan B if they don't," Allistair replied.

He didn't sound anymore thrilled about that plan than I had been. A cabin in the middle of a remote Tennessee forest. Then when she burned something down, there would hopefully be no people.

A single tendril of fear wrapped around me. Not fear for myself, but fear for what that would do to her should the wards fail. Should *we* fail. The insanity will set in and our only hope will be that it is Ruby to reason with, and not the beast.

I shuddered. If that creature were subject to the power within her while the bite of transition warped their reality...

Hell have mercy on us all.

I sent one last thundering punch into the door and the wood finally gave. A quick kick and it blew off the hinges, releasing a wave of power that even I had not predicted. The wards buckled instantly.

Fire obscured everything from view and then it died out. Nothing had burned. Nothing and no one, but the still and silent girl, crouched on her knees. Her long blue hair covered much of her naked body, but not all. Blue ivy-like vines crawled across her skin, moving and shifting like the brands she'd placed on others. It seems the transition had given her a second mark. Unheard of, but not surprising.

We waited for her to make a move.

To scream in pain.

To lash out.

Dread formed in the silence. Dread and fear.

She lifted her face and I was right to be afraid.

The wards had failed, and the beast stared back at me.

CHAPTER 7

RYSTEN WAS THE FIRST TO MOVE, TAKING A SINGLE step through the door. He watched her with caution. Like she was a wild animal.

And maybe she was, but it was too late for his caution now.

Or his pretty words.

"Why don't we go back to the room, love..." His voice trailed off when she started laughing. It began as a low husky sound. Not quite as cold as she had been in the past, but the callousness was still there.

"Do you really believe that will work on me now?" she asked him, a very self-assured smirk applied itself to her lips.

If they didn't know it yet, they were in deep shit.

"I assumed you wished to claim your next mate," Rysten said carefully. He didn't declare himself it, but he insinuated.

"There lies the problem," the beast said. She brought

her arms up over her head, cracking several joints in her body. She arched into the stretch, completely and utterly naked, only covered by a thin film of black. "You make too many assumptions. Just because she is young does not mean she cannot make choices for herself, yet you only listen when I am here."

Oh shit. I knew where this was going, but for once...I didn't really disagree.

"We do not mean to make decisions for her—"

"War," she interrupted like Rysten wasn't speaking at all. From the doorway, Laran straightened a little, but did not approach. "Do you wish to come with me, or join your brothers?"

She sounded almost bored in how she asked it, but I don't think the tone was fooling anyone. She was giving him a choice, while telling them she was leaving.

"Join my brothers?" he asked slowly. He was much better about teetering the line of respect.

"For the hunt," she supplied. He stayed still as stone, watching her with a troubled gaze.

"Don't make me do this, Ruby," his thoughts pleaded. He still didn't know we could hear.

"And you, Famine? Would you wish to join me?" the beast continued, giving nothing away.

"She intends to run," our other mate projected.

They thought they could stop her. She found this amusing.

Almost as much as the tick in Julian's jaw. At this rate, he would crack a tooth if he continued to clench so hard.

"Very well," she said after several seconds passed. "I'll be on my way, then."

A hidden smile crossed her lips as she took her first step forward and Rysten dived.

In the blink of an eye, she slammed the palm of her hand into his sternum and he went flying—straight into the mirror.

Silence filled the air until the other three registered what had just happened.

They exchanged uneasy glances, as if deciding who would try next.

Of course, with their size, the three of them couldn't all enter the bathroom and expect to fight. And while they may be born and bred warriors, the beast wasn't above playing dirty.

Allistair stepped forward and smiled, but there was nothing gentle in it.

"Little succubus," he murmured, "do you wish to play?" His voice brushed against her skin, but she wouldn't be thrown by his persuasion so easily. No matter the promise it held.

"Very much so, my golden one," she purred back, smirking with more than feminine sexuality. Allistair raised a hand, palm open, as if to offer an olive branch. She cocked her head and laughed a dark sound. "But I think we have different games in mind."

He lunged for her at the same moment she ducked. Spinning, she skated just beneath his grasp and landed a kick at his back. Allistair, too, went flying. He crashed into the bathtub, his head banging the porcelain as he did. A crack appeared and a chunk of it fell, but he looked unharmed.

The beast smirked down at him, feeling the last two enter the bathroom while she did. She couldn't see them, but she felt them. Their power. Their emotions. Their very essence called out to us. To her. She turned with a well-aimed punch to the jugular, only to hit the palm of Laran's hand. He wrapped his fingers around her fist.

"Don't make me do this, Ruby," he said, trying to pull her in. Claimed mate or not, he would try to stop her. What they all failed to see was that that's why we were in this position to begin with. I gave, and gave, and gave. I did what was asked of me. I walked away from my old life.

But I would not walk into my new one as a prisoner.

Rysten made the first move when he tried to physically subdue her.

She had washed her hands of whatever happened next, long before the first punch was thrown.

Using power I hadn't known I possessed, the beast looked up at him and leaned forward. Taking a light breath, she exhaled slowly, forming a small "O" with her lips.

Blue smoke saturated the space around him and he inhaled upon reflex, not realizing his mistake until it was too late.

"Kneel," she commanded.

And Laran—the Horseman of War—one of the most powerful beings on this world and the next—fell to his knees before his queen.

He released her hand as if compelled by whatever

spell she put on him and lowered his head in respect. She gave him a glance that no one would see. It was as close to affection as this creature could possibly get.

"You did not wish to harm me, War. I will not punish that," she murmured, just a hairsbreadth above a whisper. Laran groaned but did not move. She had full control over his actions. For how long, I wasn't sure, but I had a feeling we were going to find out.

"Please don't maim any of them. They're rather pretty how they are," I told her. The beast let out a cold laugh.

"I have no intentions of hurting that which is mine," she replied.

"Ours," I corrected.

She shrugged. To her, the semantics didn't matter. We were two beings in one body; some things were bound to be a bit difficult.

Only one now stood between her and the door.

The only one who had yet to speak.

But his silence spoke more than words could.

"Do you think you can stop me, Death, where your brothers could not?" she asked him.

He stood tall and impenetrable. His clearly defined muscles stretching beneath the thin cotton shirt. The fitted black lounge pants really accentuated his assets.

While I admired his physical traits, the beast appraised him with cool, calculating eyes. Out of all the Horsemen, he would be the hardest to get past.

Not only was he the strongest, Death was the most resistant, fighting his own attraction and the inevitable claiming.

The thought alone infuriated her, but she kept that fire close. Contained.

"Why?" he demanded, not answering the question. "Why are you doing this?"

He should have known better. His bare feet padded across the marble floors, staying just out of her reach. Circling her, but not attacking.

The beast cocked her head and watched him closely.

Trailing him where he walked was an almost invisible silver mist. It clung to his pores, brushing against his skin, filling the air with something not sweet...but sharp. Painful.

Kama.

He was giving off kama.

Did he even realize it? Did he know that he was provoking her?

They liked to talk like we were the ultimate predator. Yet, they seemed to have such a blatant disregard for these things. I was a succubus and the beast, in full transition. I wanted sex and blood and all things unholy.

But her? There was only one thing she wanted more.

She had waited twenty-three years to be let out of her cage and she had patience in spades because of it.

"I am a queen," the beast replied. "But you four seem to have forgotten that along the way. I do not exist to be put in a cage because you have deemed me too powerful. You were created to *balance* me, were you not?"

He didn't answer, but his unreadable features were slowly cracking under pressure. He liked to pull his emotions inward and bury them. To wear a mask as cold as the marble beneath her feet.

But even marble could break.

"How would you like to be put in cage? Locked in a room and told what to do? Because that's exactly what you did to us." She motioned to her own naked body.

"That was not the intent," Julian said slowly through clenched teeth.

"Intent matters not," she replied. Another fissure appeared in his armor, his emotions leaking through. He was not afraid of us. Of her. But he did feel other things.

Anger. So much anger. Unlike us, who felt fire in our belly. His wrath was cold. Desolate. All-consuming.

And right now, she was the cause of it. He wanted nothing more than to tie her up and show her what a monster he was. To lock her away from both worlds, prophecies be damned. Earth and Hell be damned. He wanted to show her what a true mate could bring and make her forget about all the humans that ever thought they could keep her. To purge them from her memory. To let her feel the bite of his teeth and the crack of a—

A barrier slammed into me, closing me off from his emotions. Julian tilted his head to the side and examined her closely.

"Ruby isn't fighting you," he murmured, more to himself than anything. "Why isn't she fighting you?"

Could he feel me in his mind? Could he sense that the beast did not hold me prisoner in my own?

She cocked her head and smiled. "There is much to be done before we return home. She knows that."

He narrowed his emerald eyes, the anger within him seeping through.

He didn't understand. None of them would. It was up to us.

I would transition and claim my mates, but the beast knew things I didn't. She could teach me things they couldn't. Make me stronger. We shared this body, and for once, our interests overlapped, even if the reasoning wasn't exactly the same.

"It's the transition. Ruby wouldn't run," Julian replied. "She knows she's safer—"

"Stop telling me what is safe!" I snapped mentally. Julian blanched like I'd struck him, and the beast smiled.

"You see, Death, I am not the only one that is tired of this. You chafe against the inevitable. You impose where it is not your duty. We want a partner. A mate. Not a bodyguard."

Without preamble, she bolted through the door, faster than Death could stop her, but not so fast that he couldn't react. She made it to the living room before he appeared in front of her, walking out of the shadows.

"There's nowhere to go and you cannot teleport," he said. Like that would stop her. Had he learned nothing? "Stop this, Ruby—"

"Why?" the beast asked, her voice turning cold. "So you can chain me up? Lock me away?" she asked mockingly, and his face darkened. He took three large steps toward us, his presence filling up the space. In his chest was a tempest of emotions, so strong, so thick that I could drown in them if not careful.

Still, she let him closer. Close enough his shirt brushed against her bare breasts. They pebbled against the friction and the ever-insistent fire burned. She looked up at him with a challenge because we weren't the only ones that had shit to work on here.

Julian stared down at her, silver particles falling from his skin. She leaned forward and inhaled deeply, a frenzy starting in her chest. His pupils dilated. Another fissure in his carefully composed mask exposed as his hard cock pressed into her belly. Her lips brushed up the hard contour of his jaw, the stubble doing deliciously wicked things to my imagination.

A growl started in his chest as he reached out and grasped her hips, pulling her closer. His control was so very close to snapping. She had every intention of letting him unravel so that we would have to put him back together. "You want me, Death?" her breath whispered across his skin, promising what was to come. "Come and get me."

The words had hardly left her lips when his hands tightened. Just as with Laran, she breathed out a heavy blue fog that he foolishly inhaled.

His hands went slack as if by command and she easily stepped out of them.

"That's a nifty trick," I said.

"I'll teach you how to do it. How to do everything, once I take care of them."

The other three Horsemen had recovered and spread themselves around the living room. Slowly closing in around her.

They muttered words in a language neither of us understood. First Laran. Then Allistair. Followed by Rysten. And Julian had regained his composure. A thread snapped around them as the four moved closer.

Binding. They were trying to *bind* her.

I wasn't sure how that possible, given what they were. None of them possessed powers to bind someone. Allistair could make me want to fuck him till I died. Laran could kill me using every element known to man. Rysten could inflict any disease on me. Julian could hold me, my spirit, between here and the veil, never allowing peace.

But none of them could bind me.

It shouldn't be possible, and yet, that is what they were about to do.

Laran withdrew a blade and sliced open his palm. Power that was not my own crackled through the air. He passed the blade to Allistair. She looked up at him with destruction in her eyes. Allistair was her second mate, but they had barely spoken on it because of the circumstances in which it came about. I could tell not by his eyes, but by his emotions, that he didn't want to do this. He didn't want to force some kind of binding on me.

But when the beast looked at him, she was not forgiving or understanding.

He sighed under his breath in frustration, but at least had the balls to look at her as he brought the knife down. Blue blood splattered the carpet and the air popped around her, almost like a vacuum. She could hear nothing but them and their whispers as it slowly rose to a chant.

Rysten took the knife next, his eyes speaking an apology that his mouth would not say. She stared back at him defiantly and he cringed as he slashed his hand. Blood swirled, moving to form a circle around her. All it took was one and the binding would be complete.

She moved to knock the knife away and hit an invisible barrier.

I grimaced, but she was not perturbed. The beast had an ace up her sleeve that no one, not even I, had realized.

She felt for his presence and called to him.

They could not stop her. No one could.

Not when she had her familiars.

From down the hall a wild screech rang out as twenty pounds of fur and fury launched itself towards us. Bandit had been waiting and answer the call, he did.

He leapt through the barrier that was meant for her, and she leaned down for him to scurry up her arm.

She summoned a circle of flame around them and forced it outwards. The two magics clashed together at the edge of the circle and the fire swayed. They were strong. Strong enough that without Bandit she might not have been able to do it.

His claws pricked her skin, the sharp pain filling her with a sociopathic sort of calm.

She ground her nails in the palms of her hands and the sweltering heat within us snapped, sending a pulsing wave of fire at their circle.

The blood incinerated, and the binding broke as the flames of Hell consumed it all. The Horsemen were thrown from where they stood by the immense power that erupted from within her.

She stepped out of the blood circle and I made note of the magic they had used.

Magic that I had only seen once before.

Magic that demons could not use.

My attention focused on the scene before me as she

looked over her shoulder and blew them a kiss. Blue flames burned at their clothes, but the Horsemen were unharmed, albeit furious as they watched her.

None more so than Death.

"If you want us, then you will earn us."

She turned back to the wall of glass and took off at a run.

It exploded on impact and melted before it could cut her skin. The wall of glass that had kept us in was ultimately the weakest point, allowing us our freedom.

Stark naked, she jumped from the third story of the apartment building and landed with a victory cry from Bandit.

Without a glance back at what we'd left behind, the beast and Bandit walked into the shadows of New Orleans and she whispered into the dead of night, "Let the games begin."

LARAN

Shattered glass and black ash. The fleeting scent of amaryllis and old magic. Ruby hadn't just left us. She'd destroyed us. She and the beast.

It gave me a choice, to stay or to go. I chose wrong.

At the time, I didn't think she would get further than ten feet. That one of us would catch her.

But no one did, and now she was smoke in the wind.

Burnt carpet and the tang of blood filled the air in her stead. It was all that remained of our failed attempt to not only catch Ruby, but to contain her as well.

"We have to go after her," Death growled.

"No fucking kidding," Allistair spat.

They were angry. They should be. I should be...and yet, I wasn't.

As a claimed mate to the daughter of the devil, I was privy to some things. Brief flashes of emotion. A sense of knowing. Our bond was only half formed with a fraction of her own magic placed beneath my skin. Nothing near

93

the amount Moira should feel as her familiar, but a small sliver of that wild magic lay there. Pulling me. Prodding me.

Even from far away I could sense the panic inside of her. The turbulent emotions were more reminiscent of a firestorm, as opposed to the pure lust a succubus should feel in transition. She was upset, and something told me we were the ones who caused it.

I sighed deeply, walking to the edge. Glass crunched beneath my bare feet as I looked out over New Orleans, but the dark city kept its secrets and hid my transitioning mate.

We had to find her. They weren't wrong.

But we had to make it right.

I turned away from the glass and walked through the house. The other Horsemen did not follow me. I was not their concern, not now, not ever.

A single unmarked door sat at the end of a hallway.

I did not delay.

The metal of the handle was hot, but not as heated as the room inside. Nothing was ablaze, apart from the wings of a sleeping girl. She lay on her back with her flaming wings spread limply across the bed. Arms strewn across her chest and head lying at an angle, the pinched expression of her face did not make me think she was having happy dreams.

I looked to the ceiling knowing that once I did this, it was done. There was no going back. I was waking a sleeping monster, quite literally, who may be as powerful as me for all we knew.

But she was my mate's familiar, and if anyone could bring her back to us, it was this girl and only her.

"Moira," I said her name once and that was all it took. The banshee's eyes flew wide open. Glazed and unfocused, she stared at the ceiling for a moment.

"What have you done?"

CHAPTER 8

I don't know what in Satan's name I was thinking giving her control, but it's not like there was much I could do about it now. With my out of control magic and never-ending fever, we were safer with her in charge. As odd as that may sound. She at least knew how to control the flames. That was more than could be said for me. Last time I tried, the best I could manage was *not* spreading the fire and my track record wasn't exactly stellar.

Bandit let out a chittering noise, drawing my attention to them because she was heading into a pretty shady part of town. Covered by nothing more than a thin film of obsidian ash, the beast strutted forth with a self-assured confidence, paying no mind to those on the street who passed her.

"Where are you going?" I probably should have asked that before now, but I guess it was better late than never.

"I'm hungry." Umm...there was two ways to construe

that and I wasn't very comfortable with either. *"I expended a lot of energy breaking the binding."*

The binding they shouldn't have been able to create as demons. Best not to forget that. Only the Unseelie had blood magic, and while the Horsemen weren't any old demons, they weren't Fae either. Something wasn't adding up here.

"How were they able to cast that in the first place?" I wondered.

"I don't know." Her body did not react, but I sensed her displeasure. Not with me, but with the unknown. With the things that neither of us knew or understood because of the roles we'd played for twenty-three years. Her, the prisoner waiting to be released. Me, the ignorant half-demon that didn't want to believe the truth when it bailed me out of jail. Neither roles left us well-equipped for what we would become. Good thing I was a quick study and she could simply use brute force.

She rounded a corner, ignoring the damp air that embraced her like a lover. It may have been December, but we weren't in Oregon any more. Here you didn't just drink your water. You inhaled it. And judging by the thick clouds looming in the night sky, tonight was going to pour. The wispy base of the clouds lit in shades of purple and pink from light pollution, casting a glow over the crescent city. Meanwhile, soft music drifted from somewhere in the distance. Calling to us.

The beast lifted her head and parted her lips, inhaling the stray gust of wind that broke through the heavy atmosphere. Scents of sweat and blood filled her nostrils, along with something else...the barest hint of kama.

"Dinner," she surmised, following the wind. It led in the same direction as the music.

"I'm not fucking anyone but the four males we left back there, so if that's your great plan—" I started to protest.

"We're not fucking anyone," the beast replied. She didn't give any further explanation as to what we were doing, but as long as I was in the backseat, I guess the best I could do was watch.

She strolled through the brightly lit streets with purpose, tracking that infinitesimal fleck of kama. Several men hooted and hollered, women too, but she paid them no mind. As Allistair would say, they were beneath her attention.

The beast purred at the thought of him. Not because she missed him. Oh no. She was more fucked up than that. She purred at the fact that they were probably going out of their minds trying to find us, because she wanted them to earn their spot. It was going to be a fun game of cat and mouse as they tried to catch us, and she repeatedly slipped through their fingers.

They wouldn't catch her and keep her until they got smarter and learned we would go where we pleased. That we wouldn't be locked away.

We could hold our own in every way and they needed to fucking realize that.

She laughed as she came to a halt in front of a door. Outside, two men—no, two demons—stood with their arms over their chests. A line wrapped around the block, consisting of both humans and demons. Internally I frowned, until I realized the only people they were turning away at the door were humans.

She glanced up, a smirk coming over her lips at the name of the club.

The Lotus.

This sounded like a bad idea if I ever heard one.

"Are you sure you know what you're doing here?"

Instead of answering me, she walked up to the front of the line and took a slow breath. This was indeed the place. Kama flowed into our lungs, both sating the succubus side and luring her deeper. My thoughts scattered, slipping through my grasp as I tried to cling to a reason for why we shouldn't enter.

Not that the beast cared whether I did or didn't have a reason. She walked forward to stand at the rope, and both the bouncers, as well as most of the line, took notice. Hard not to when there's a naked girl covered in glittery black shit.

I really hoped she chose to find us some clothes soon, because the two large blokes looked like they might eat me.

"What do we have here—"

"Move," the beast cut him off. There was such darkness in her tone. An inkling as to what they would find if they disobeyed.

The larger of the two demons peered down at her, his glamor non-existent to her eyes. Bright red skin and a tail. He was a rare form of monster, exceptionally useful for guarding things, but not the smartest of demons. The rubrum were born with skin the color of bone, but as they proved their battle prowess and bathed in their enemies' blood, it gradually turned red or blue, absorbing the pigment. Judging by his skin at this unknown hour in the night, I'd say he was middle of the way.

That his skin was red and not blue like demons' blood spoke volumes as to what most of his kills were. The beast did not shy away.

The rubrum was not who answered her, though, but instead an imp with hard features and a vicious smile. He didn't know that we had history with his kind, and that if he didn't watch himself, he'd end up Bar-B-Que. Or raccoon food. It was a toss-up at this point.

"That's not how it works, little lady."

Why was it that males loved to use pet names? I sighed internally, and the beast cocked her head.

"You will move, one way or another."

With that, she held up her hand where both humans and demons could see and snapped her fingers. A small blue flame appeared, spreading to her fingertips. She took a step forward and the imp took a step back. That made her smile.

The humans started running.

The demons in line had the good sense to either back away slowly or stay still, lowering their gaze in a sign of submission.

"Whoa...we didn't mean—"

"I know what you meant."

Bandit's claws pricked at her arms as he arched forward and let out a growl. Clearly, he wasn't a fan of the demon either.

Fortunately for them, that was the moment the imp

decided to make this easy. He unclipped the rope and stepped aside, lowering his head slightly. The beast walked forward and unflinchingly gazed up at the rubrum who was still trying to decide whether he should attempt to take us on. The imp elbowed him in the side and flicked his eyes down, trying to give the other bouncer the hint.

She waited, her eyes staring past the black irises of the lesser demon, straight into the fiery pits of his soul.

Broken loves and stinging losses filled the empty void in front of us where the rubrum stood. His soul was marked by pain that was used in an attempt to make him pliant.

Abuse. He suffered from extreme abuse at the hands of other demons. The beast took this in, staring at the angry red light from within his chest. While my own internal light was a bright blue that flickered like flames, his was dark. Dangerous. The rubrum were a loyal lot, but someone had hurt this one inexplicably.

I don't know what possessed her to do what she did next. That's not true. I knew it was me. What I didn't know was that I possessed any power over her. However, it seemed that our body was always at odds in trying to balance us, and neither one was completely in control.

Either way, I acted on instinct, just like I had with Moira. Leaning forward, I pushed the beast to place her hand on his chest, driven by an urge I didn't understand and had no hope of controlling.

Her fire-tipped fingers splayed across the cheap material, burning straight through his tight t-shirt. The rubrum did not scream or lift a hand against her. He was better trained than that. His muscles clenched tightly as the fire licked at his chest. She pushed the heat inward to burn at the festering wounds around his soul. It hurt more in the moment as the fire burned away the dead and dying parts. I could sense his pain, feel it, searing through his chest. He thought he was being splayed open before the world, but really, the demons around us had no idea.

Fire was destructive. Deadly. But if used right, fire could heal. As the most brutal form of cleansing, it had the power to wipe clean the stains. Our fire ate through the diseased parts of his soul that held him down, cauterizing wounds that were slowly killing him.

He burned in an inferno that others couldn't see.

And then it was done.

The beast pulled away, not bothering to avert her eyes from the charred handprint she left on his chest. But there was no pentagram like there had been with the others she'd claimed. The beast was careful to heal, but not to bond in any way.

Which was good. The Horsemen might've killed him if they thought otherwise.

The beast stepped away and turned for the door, even more depleted than when she'd walked up. Internally, she was grumbling something about me being allowed to make requests. It wasn't her I was really listening to.

"Hey—hey—" A warm hand wrapped around her arm. She turned slowly, her dark gaze falling on him like the chill of death. The rubrum had the good sense to drop his hand. An almost sheepish look crossed his face as he sank to both knees before her. "You...you healed me. How can I repay you?"

The beast stared on impassively. "You have nothing I desire."

The rubrum frowned, running his hand across his five o'clock shadow. "Nothing?"

His brows inched up as she repeated, "Nothing."

I didn't get the impression he was used to other demons not wanting anything from him. That's how it was with most of our kind.

"That won't do," he mumbled, his tail shifting back and forth as he frowned to himself, thinking in silence. "Surely there's something I can give..." He trailed off, almost like he was distraught. I hadn't met any rubrum before, but he definitely wasn't panning out like the stereotypes.

The beast cocked her head, pursing her lips. "What do they call you?" she asked.

"What do they call you? Really? This is the twenty-first century. No one talks like that," I sniped at her. She didn't reply.

"The name's Eugene McGee. My friends call me Gene," the rubrum answered, almost chipper. That was...unexpected.

"I need to replenish and then I need a guide. Do you think you could handle that, Eugene McGee?" she asked him in her heartless voice. I wanted to bang my head against the wall, but it would do no good. Whatever power I momentarily took from her to heal him was already gone and she was firmly in control with a plan that was batshit crazy on a good day.

"They're going to go insane looking for us. You know that, right?" I asked her. The beast smiled outwardly as Eugene McGee got to his feet to escort her in, ignoring the annoying imp who couldn't stop gawking.

"I'm planning on it," she replied as she stepped into the strip club.

When they finally caught up, she had every intention of going with them, but that didn't mean she was going to make it easy. She'd waited a long time for this, and she was going to make the most of it.

MOIRA

"You did *what*?" I snapped at them, momentarily trans-fixed as the words left my mouth...like a ripple on a lake, the tenor pushed outwards and towards the walls.

The room strained beneath the tension. I blinked.

"Moira, we need your help right now—"

I tilted my head. His voice also gave off waves, but these were flexible, not hard or unyielding as mine were. I reached out to touch the almost invisible bending of light and sound.

The wave parted, and a dual echo filled my ears.

Strange...

"You were saying," I murmured. Again, a ripple filled the air. Like the sun in a desert, the longer I stared at the distant wall in front of me, the more the ripples contin-ued. They hit the walls in front of me, flattening with a ping against the hard surface.

"The beast is free in New Orleans—"

The almost invisible bending lines followed the

direction of his voice. I pushed them backwards wanting to shove them down his throat at the obscenity of that statement.

And guess what?

They did.

The taut tendrils snapped and raced back inside of him. Laran—tall, broad, and strong as he was—clutched his throat in pain.

I smiled cruelly.

"You lost her?" I asked, this time focusing on War and not the power coursing in my veins, or the way the air practically sang.

There was sound in *everything*.

And I had power over sound.

"We didn't lose her," he ground out with a rough growl. I gave him a non-amused look and pushed those waves back inside of him. Harder.

The asshole choked, and I didn't feel the least bit bad.

I couldn't remember much before sleeping. Ruby had been having one of her Debbie downer moments and I told her to get over herself. Fuck them, brand them, and be done with it.

We didn't have time for anything else.

Clearly, she had deviated a bit from that, somewhere along the way.

"You're awake?"

The sound came from a different dumbass. I whipped my head around, relinquishing whatever hold I had over the ripples that caused Laran pain.

"Obviously." My voice cut through the air like a

scythe. Sharper than any blade, and it was well below a scream or a shout.

I was quite surprised when a crack split the air as it ran through the wall beside him. I arched an eyebrow, because that was just too fucking convenient to be anything but me. But I was just a banshee, and a half-breed at that...

But the wall had cracked.

And Laran had choked.

And Rysten was pale as a sheet.

"I'm assuming he told you then?" He flicked his eyes to Laran. Not quite angry, but also not kind. He hadn't wanted me awakened.

Awakened...

Why did that sound so—I reached for my chest gasping for a tight breath, because I remembered. I remembered *everything*. The burning. The tear. The ripping in my back as my muscles were torn apart. The scorch as the flames ran through my blood, filling every nook and cranny with a volatile magic. It filled my very being, mixing with everything that I am.

It fused with me. Molded to me. Changed me.

The feeling of a knife carving into my forehead sent a fresh wave of anxiety as I rode the memory, lost in a flashback.

There was a heavy aching in my back where a weight that shouldn't be there sat like a log. I reached out to brush the sweat from my forehead and pull the tangled hairs away from my face. My hand snagged on something sharp.

I pulled away. Blood. A thin line of blue blood ran

down a cut in my palm. I frowned at the trickle of sapphire, and then I reached again.

Horns.

I had fucking *horns*.

Should I have been upset? Because an almost gleeful feeling began to fill me.

I turned and caught a glimpse of something large and blue and made of...*flame*.

Wings.

Those were *wings*. And they were attached to my back.

I had wings. I had horns. I was seeing waves in the air —and controlling them, for that matter.

But most of all, there was an incessant tugging in my chest. An invisible line that led from me straight to my blue-haired best friend. I'd felt attached to her before. She was my family after all, and apparently, I was her familiar. This was something different, though, and a sneaking suspicion sat on the edge of my mind. I grasped for it, trying to piece every bit of information that I held. Like smoke, it slipped through my grasp, but I wouldn't give up so easily.

Something wasn't right here.

"What am I?"

Rysten blanched. Laran sighed.

They were feeling nervous now? Shy all of a sudden, *after* they woke me up? I didn't wait for them to start rambling. I pushed my way out of the door and walked down the hallway, passing both Julian and Allistair as I turned for the bathroom—and stopped dead in my tracks.

Black ashes. Broken glass. A mirror splintered into a million pieces.

There, in all the shards, was my reflection refracted a thousand different ways. I leaned over, aware of the silence as I picked up a single fragment of mirror and looked at myself.

A horned helmet atop two black wings.

The mark of Cain.

And it was branded on my forehead.

Well, well, well. It seems that somehow, in some way, I had transitioned.

"Alright pony boys, it's time you start talking and tell me how the fuck I became a legion." Pestilence choked on a cough.

"And then, we're going to figure out how to get Ruby back."

CHAPTER 9

THE DAYS BLURRED AS WE TRAVELED FROM ONE CLUB to the next, feeding on the kama in the atmosphere. True to her word, we didn't screw a single person—but as the days went by, I was itching to. We were still very much in transition, and while she seemed to be able to control it, the brief moments I had peeked through only resulted in...small catastrophes...or miracles. It really depended on how you looked at it.

Eugene McGee was the only demon whose soul I healed, but he was far from the only odd case of magical output. On the first night in the Lotus, she ended up so high that I slipped in momentarily and ended up turning Bandit's hair blue. Not that he seemed to mind being ringed in black and blue. If I didn't know any better, I'd say he thought he looked rather stylish. He certainly seemed to be flaunting himself more, but that may just have been the steady diet of fresh fish Eugene was bringing him. The rubrum seemed to feel that he owed me a life debt, and no request the beast made, no matter how outlandish, swayed him to thinking otherwise. He'd decided our well-being was of the utmost importance, and while I could almost find it sweet at times—the hero worship didn't sit well with me. Not to mention how the Horsemen would react when they did catch up.

Red lights pulsed through the club, lighting up the stage and casting the strippers in a dark glow. The Devil's Dancers was packed tonight, filled with naked demons of both sexes, catering to all tastes. The kama that the audience was putting off was keeping us fed and alert. Her body tingled against the colored particles that pressed against her skin, slowly slipping beneath it. It kept us calm, but the need for sex was beginning to heighten, and the beast wasn't happy the Horsemen hadn't gotten their shit together yet. I mean, how hard could it be for them to find a blue-haired she-demon dressed in a stripper's get-up? In New Orleans? The answer was it was like finding a needle in a haystack.

She leaned back, crossing her legs where the thigh-highs stopped. She'd asked Eugene to bring her clothes at some point and he came back with an itty bitty dress, complete with thigh-highs and hooker heals. While it garnered more attention than necessary, it also made it easy to get into the demon clubs he brought us to. Everyone was dressed kind of sleazy and it was often difficult to distinguish the strippers from the guests.

The beast looked on, ignoring the sweltering fever that made her body slick with sweat. Her skin clung to the vinyl chair, uncomfortably so. Not that anyone could tell when they saw her. Where the heat had driven me to violent extremes, she was able to take it all in stride.

Her stare was unflinching as she examined the crowd before her. Demons were fickle creatures. One moment they could be partaking in an orgy without a care as to who watched them. The next they could be ripping each other's throats out while still balls deep in one another. It was a gut-wrenching sight, filled with savageness and primal instinct. Humans called us evil. I could see where that notion came from. We were not of this world. Me. The beast. Any demon or Fae. We didn't come from here.

We didn't belong here.

That was a thought that seemed to be running through my head more and more as of late. Maybe it was because of the fire in my veins, or the quite literal desire to start burning shit. Maybe it was because I was beginning to harden further to the world, sinking deeper into the monster I was becoming. Or maybe the more I looked, the more savageness appealed to me in a way that human conventions never did.

While I'd run from the demons on earth before, I was never really normal. I never blended perfectly with the humans. The slew of stalker exes and my mile-long rap sheet were proof of that. I was only ever biding time.

Similar to how the beast was now.

"I'm not biding my time," she grumbled. Her moods were already crappy enough. This game wasn't making them better.

"You're waiting for the Horsemen to find us," I snorted.

She grimaced outwardly while Bandit stretched out

on her lap. He wore a tiny cone-shaped party hat attached by a stretchy string. Where he got it, neither of us knew, only that he insisted on wearing it.

"I'm letting them learn an important lesson," she replied. I suppose that was one way to look at it. *"One that you agreed with,"* she continued.

Now it was my turn to grumble inwardly. That put a smirk on her lips.

"Yes...no...I don't know. You haven't exactly put us in an easy situation and it's not like we're doing much." I muttered the last bit. Not like that kept it from her. She knew every thought and feeling I had, as much as I knew hers in return. So when the strange combination of humor and annoyance swirled in her chest, I found myself dreading what would come next.

"You're bored," she said pointedly.

No. Maybe...I tried to squelch down any reaction and it only served to intensify her emotions more.

"I was pissed at them in the beginning, but I got over it," I started, mentally fumbling when I could feel her growing agitation. The truth was that I was mad. Now I wasn't, and we were in a city crawling with demons, with no back-up if and when shit went sideways—apart from Bandit. While my raccoon was awesome...he wasn't from Hell. He didn't have powers. He just knew how to bite the shit out of someone while I started burning things up.

"You're being emotional about this," she replied coldly.

Emotional? The beast wanted to talk to me about being emotional?

"Says the person who is running all over the city in

some fucked up game of hide-and-seek because they got a bit controlling after we threw Laran through a wall," I quipped back at her. She seemed to consider this for a moment, slowly stroking her fingers through Bandit's thick fur while watching an orgy taking place in front of us.

"You agreed," she settled on eventually. I sighed, wanting to shake my head at her, but I wasn't in control.

"Yes, and I don't regret that. I'm just saying we could be doing more than sitting around and waiting to get abducted...again."

The beast snorted. Yup. Actually snorted. I wouldn't have believed it if I hadn't known with absolute certainty. Just like that, her anger was gone, replaced by mild amusement and weary agreement.

She arched forward, and a smacking sound filled the air as the vinyl that had been sticking to her back released. Sweat clung to her skin like a layer of clothing, insulating the heat within. The burning was beginning to get out of control, but the beast hadn't cracked. She wouldn't. While the sweat may be annoying, she was a creature of the flames confined by a mortal body. Soon to be more. The heat within didn't just come from her. It *was* her.

So, suffer I would, and I counted my lucky stars she was taking the brunt of it instead of me.

She hauled herself out of the armchair, waving down Eugene with a single look. He caught her watchful eye and nodded, pushing his way through the orgy to come to her.

"Ruby, what is it?" he asked, a slight frown forming.

He'd been nothing but attentive to her every demand since we'd healed his soul. I wonder if he realized exactly who he was dealing with, or if he just didn't care. I was leaning towards ignorance given the lack of fear, but that could just be because she saved him, and he thinks he's safe.

No one was safe. Not unless you wore her brand.

"I'm bored. Find me somewhere more interesting."

To Eugene's credit, he kept his face neutral and didn't balk at the unreasonableness behind her request. We both knew why she was bored.

She didn't want to be in a dingy bar watching other demons fuck.

She wanted to be fucking *our* mates. Of course, getting her to admit that was like getting Bandit to eat brussels sprouts. Not fucking happening.

"There's a—"

A scream rang through the air, cutting him off. Her muscles tensed. That wasn't just any scream. It was a banshee's scream.

Adrenaline surged within her as she searched for the source. Bodies pressed in around her. Their slick skin brushing against hers as she pushed her way through the crowd, quickly growing impatient. While most people possessed a sense of fight or flight, the beast only contained one mode and limited emotions, extreme as they might be.

She elbowed a male demon in the stomach that stepped too close for our liking, letting out a threatening snarl. Another bout of screams erupted to her right. Her head whipped around, and her muscles trembled as she took in the scene before her.

The banshee wasn't Moira. Thankfully.

They all might have died if it was.

While she shared her scream and dark green locks, their faces looked nothing alike. Moira burned like the fire inside me. This she-demon was completely and utterly terrified of the two males that had her trapped. Blood leaked from both their ears, dripping down their shoulders. Despite the damage she'd inflicted on them, one stood at her back, using his arms to cage her while he painfully squeezed her bare breasts. The other stood in front, flush against her body, playing with something between them...

Thick and dangerous, rage wrapped around our chest when we saw the shredded panties in his hand.

The banshee let out a raspy scream. Her voice broke as the demons around us watched with lust in their eyes. She writhed in their arms, throwing her head back in an attempt to smash her attacker's nose. He dodged last second, leaning forward to bite her neck in warning.

The beast didn't hesitate where all other demons did. She walked forward with vengence in her eyes and fire at her command.

"Help me!" the girl cried, meeting our eyes over his shoulder. Up close, the tears running down her face were making an awful mess of her make-up, but without all the gunk on her face, she looked young.

The beast's face remained impassive as she reached out, wrapping a burning hand around the male's shoulder. He let out a roar, throwing his weight back in an attempt to break her grip. She wasn't having any of it.

The beast turned her finger's claw-like, digging into his leather skin. He groaned in pain as she shredded through the muscle and tendons, crushing him straight to the bone.

"You like to gang rape unprotected demons?" she asked him. At some point the club had quieted so only labored breathing and "Sweet Dreams" could be heard. "Because I like to hurt those that deserve it." She wrenched him down to eye level using the unnatural strength I never could get under control. "Do you deserve it?"

He gave a grunt of pain and black spikes popped out of his skin. Chupacabra.

"Listen, bitch, I don't know what—"

She slapped him so hard his neck cracked.

"Wrong answer."

That blow would have killed a human, but instead it left his head hanging at an odd angle as his body rapidly tried to heal itself. She threw him ten feet, his back snapping as he hit the stage at a bad angle. One of his spikes shot from his skin, aiming for her chest. She caught it in one hand and turned, slamming it into the remaining rapist's shoulder. His arms convulsed around the small banshee as the poison instantly started to spread.

"You...you..." His words faded as his veins turned black beneath his paper white skin. His eyes rolled to the back of his head as he stumbled, his legs now struggling to hold him. The young banshee looked between us, unsure if she had traded one danger for another.

The beast turned her eyes back on the chupacabra. His pain turned to rage as he looked away from his friend's steadily weakening form and back to the beast.

He didn't use words before he came at her, moving faster than she expected with his body broken. Still, that didn't stop her. He swiped an arm in her direction—letting loose three spikes. She acted without hesitation, summoning a wall of hellfire to extinguish the poisonous spikes before they could touch her.

That was when the screaming started. Not from the banshee beside her, but the monsters standing on the sidelines. Not many things could kill a demon flat out, but the flames of Hell were one of them.

Quickly tiring of the games, she strode forward through the fire, relishing how it licked at her skin. The chupacabra didn't run. He didn't fight. He simply watched the fire behind her, knowing that if she wished him dead, there was nothing he could do to stop her.

"Who are you?" he whispered, swallowing hard as she approached him. She grasped his naked cock as it hung limp between his thighs like a broken toy.

"Evil's executioner."

There was a wicked glint in her eye as she castrated him by fire. He was curled into a ball of agony when she moved onto the demon lying comatose from the poisonous spike she had impaled him with. He didn't even have time to beg before his appendage was removed by flame.

And then it was finished. Well, Bandit ran up and pissed on him for good measure, but the damage was done.

All she was left with was the wide-eyed she-demon she'd saved, Eugene McGee's troubled expression, and a roomful of demons that fell to their knees. They were bowing...to their queen.

The banshee blinked twice before dropping onto her knees. This didn't sit right with me, but the beast didn't seem to care. At the very least, they were showing the respect she felt she deserved.

Selfish cunt.

Of course, before she could say anything to the lot of them, two very familiar faces stepped out of the shadows.

Rysten...and Julian.

They'd come for her. For us.

Finally.

Unfortunately, this little turn of events had her blood pumping. The beast rather liked taking a more proactive role in getting scumbags off the street. Doling out punishments as she saw fit. If they had come not ten minutes earlier, she might have gone.

But now... now she had plans. Ideas.

If the Horsemen couldn't catch her, she had every intention of following them through. She let out a whistle and Bandit scurried across the stone floor, leaping halfway up her body and climbing the rest of the way. He perched on her shoulder, growling at them on principle. They weren't Laran. This didn't surprise me.

"Ruby," Julian growled under his breath. The look he gave her...it made me shiver. If he caught her, there was no way he was letting her go. Over his dead body, and considering I was pretty sure he couldn't die...

"Death," the beast purred with the voice of a siren.

The vein in his temple bulged as he took her in, skimpy dress and all.

"Come now, love. We've won the game. Time to go." Rysten prowled in the shadows of the room, jumping from spot to spot, slowly getting closer to her. She threw her head back and let out a wicked laugh.

"You've found me, Pestilence, but you've yet to win."

She turned to Eugene McGee and nodded once. He took two steps.

Rysten needed three.

But they were already gone, falling through the floor beneath them.

RYSTEN

My arms wrapped around air. Hot. Sweaty. But ultimately empty air.

I stopped where I stood and looked down at the spot where the beast and some rubrum had been. A sinking sensation in my gut said I'd fucked up. Not only had I been the one to release her from the wards and lose her the first time, I'd also been the one to deviate from the plan and fail a second time.

"Where is she?" Julian roared.

I didn't flinch against the brutal thrust of power that swept through the room, searching for the missing she-demon. If they had been invisible, he would have found her, but the beast and the rubrum were not here. That almighty power that Julian released turned fraught and chaotic with the sharp bite of cold.

Demons hated the cold, but Julian embraced it.

I grit my teeth against his rage and kept a tight leash on my own power. If I let loose the sickness that ate away inside of me, the room of demons would die a very painful death and Julian would take it as challenge with the state he was in. All of our existence he'd been not just the strongest, but the most rational. Ever since we'd found Ruby, his controlling nature and tortured mind had begun to unravel. The beast walking out seemed to have brought out the worst in both of them, and while I had every intention of killing that rubrum with her when I found them—losing my temper would not be a wise idea.

So, I did what I was best at.

I dropped my arms and settled all of the darkness deep inside me where my brother couldn't see it. I would go hunting when he was asleep to get it out of my system. I turned my face, hiding the emotions I had a more difficult time keeping from him. In his primal state, he wouldn't even notice I was doing it. Ruby was the first who ever had.

"She's gone, Julian. I went too early and she ran before Moira could even attempt to calm her down." Honesty. It worked best for him in situations like this.

"She can't just be gone," he hissed.

The darker side of his magic clung to him more and more as the years went by, making him more like the beast than he ever would admit.

"We need to get the banshee and track her down before she goes too far." That was my only reply before I turned my thoughts to Allistair. Before I could reach out to him, something smashed against my face. I turned and spat blood across the club floor. It mixed with the blood the beast had painted this place in, and the urge to kill someone filled me again. Harder to control this time, when I recognized my attacker.

"What the fuck was that?" Laran bellowed.

I popped my unhinged jaw back into place and gave him a level stare.

"I saw an opportunity and I took it—" He hit me again.

I coughed hoarsely, spewing droplets of blood across the damn place. On the other side of me, Julian didn't say a fucking word, leaving me to deal with the anger of War alone. Maybe he wanted to hit me too, so this was him giving me a chance to at least fight back. I wouldn't.

"Listen, mate," I paused to rip out a tooth that was half hanging on by a chunk of gum. The new one was already pushing through. "I fucked up, but—"

His fist slammed into my face a third time, and I roared back in response. That tight hold I kept on myself strained for a moment, as my power itched to unleash an even worse fate on the hotheaded asshole. Pain like broken teeth and missing limbs were often easier for people to handle than a wasting sickness that ate them alive from within. I saw it every day with humans, and we demons—we were no different.

It took me a moment to recover from that one, staring at the shiny concrete floor, my face a mass of broken bone and flesh was healing rapidly. When I could move my lips I said, "Do not hit me again."

It would be the only warning. He had the right to be pissed, and I would even grant him the first punch for breaking the plan and trying to talk to her myself. I thought I could fix what I had done. I was wrong, but I would only grant him so much before he got a taste of the rot that lurked within.

"You broke formation. Moira was moving in, and *you* spooked her."

His fists were a pain that I could take. It was his words that cut me because I already knew it was my fault. That my actions blew the chance we had.

"Moira can still track her," I said. Like she'd done a dozen times already, just for the beast to cause some kind of havoc and disappear before we even saw her.

"Actually..." a fourth voice interjected. Allistair stepped out from behind the stage. Moira wasn't with him. "She can't. After you blew the plan, the banshee decided that she was better off doing the job on her own."

Fire and ice clashed as both Julian and Laran turned hostile.

"She said that?" Laran demanded.

"I believe her words were, *if I want it done right, I should do it myself.*"

"You let her leave." Julian's words were hardly more than a growl. His own sanity was beginning to fray at the edges.

"I attempted to persuade her to stay and she somehow redirected it. By the time I could break my own persuasion, she had decided flying was the best way to leave without me being able to follow."

Fuck.

This just kept going from bad to worse. I knew the banshee was not thrilled with us, but I didn't exactly expect her to follow through on her threats. Son of a bitch. If the beast gets both of her familiars, and is left unchecked, New Orleans will burn.

"There has to be another way to find her," I said. "Something—someone that can track her—"

"We need more than just to be able to track her." There was a dark note in Julian's tone.

"We won't be able to bind her if she has both of her familiars," Allistair said.

"More than a binding," Julian answered.

"Are you suggesting—" Allistair started, and there was a heavy warning in his voice. A flicker of unease, because what Julian wanted to do to her...not even I would be willing to face her ire when she found out. Ruby would forgive a lot, but this? Julian was too far gone.

"I am."

He was going to get our girl back, no matter the cost.

CHAPTER 10

HER ASS SMACKED ONTO THE COLD, HARD GROUND and Bandit let out a mewling sound. Techno music blared in the background, adding to the disorienting stars exploding in front of her. She growled, waiting for the world to stop spinning before attempting to sit up. Pulling herself to an upright position, she ignored her protesting muscles. We were still mortal after all, and that wasn't a short fall. Bandit clung to her chest, wrapping his arms tightly around her neck like he was hanging on for dear life. He probably was.

The ceiling had to be a good twelve feet or more above us. She glanced around the room, taking note of the pool table to our side and sheer number of...men. Human men. Many of which seemed to have better dance moves than me.

After observing the shadowed corners, she quickly got to her feet, turning to look for Eugene. He stood a few feet behind her, cloaked by glamor to look like a beautiful dark-skinned man with long, luscious hair. I wanted to ask why he chose that particular look, but the beast didn't give a shit. She just wanted a way out of here.

"C'mon. I know a back door." He jerked his head to the hallway cloaked in shadow. While it was the ideal place for Rysten or Julian to grab her, it was less obvious than the front door. They turned and headed for the dark hallway, ignoring the catcalls some of the men made as she walked by.

"Hey, sweet thang," someone rumbled behind her. She turned her head, hand curled inward just itching to have another castrating session—something I didn't agree with down here unless someone made a move. But the dimpled man wasn't looking at her...

Eugene flushed a purple hue beneath his glamor, tipped his chin and kept on walking.

At the end of the corridor, a metal door opened up into an alley with a screech, slamming shut behind her with an audible click.

Outside, the night was chilly, pleasantly so. She trailed after Eugene, ignoring his odd behavior as they made their way through the darker parts of New Orleans that tourists didn't go to. Here you only walked around outside if you were brave, stupid, or a demon. Those labels weren't mutually exclusive.

After stumbling on the uneven pavement for what seemed like the umpteenth time that night, the beast paused and tore off the seven-inch hooker heels we'd been wearing for days. I was already tall, and while I wouldn't consider myself uncoordinated, I didn't exactly wear heels if I had *any* other choice, and that was in the best possible conditions. Certainly not on these terribly maintained streets. The beast must have shared that sentiment since she ripped them off her feet and chucked them down an alley. Eugene paused at the end of the street and didn't comment when she caught up. It was smart of him. Good survival instincts.

We walked another five minutes in the stifling silence before a creeping feeling had the hairs along the back of our neck prickling. She stopped walking.

"Everything alright?" Eugene asked, concern edging his voice.

The beast watched him for a hard moment before turning her gaze to the decrepit buildings. Nothing *looked* out of the ordinary, but still she stared a few seconds longer at the darkest of the shadows.

A distinct feeling of unease filled us, and the urge to run.

But there was nothing there.

She turned to continue walking when she saw it.

The thing moved like darkness, absorbing all light that it touched. Its eyes were the color of lava, red and angry. Molten with rage. Animalistic fury.

My mind formed what her mouth would not.

Hellhound.

The thing raised its head, snarling a breath across the twenty meters that separated us. It smelled like fire and ash. Death and decay.

But did the beast run?

No, she fucking didn't.

She stared at it like an equal, not even willing to lower her eyes. Bandit arched his back and let out a hiss, like that was going to scare the damn thing off. I could have sworn the hellhound tilted its head and let out a low growl. A sharp whistle cut through the air, and the hound sat back on its haunches. Each of its four legs alone had to be ten feet tall. The head was the size of my old VW bug, with a pointed snout and ears that sat straight up like a Doberman.

"Eugene!" a man called out of the shadows. "Well, if it isn't Eugene McGee."

No, not a man: a demon. For the second time in my life, I saw a rubrum. Tall and imposing. He stood a good eight feet tall with skin so dark it looked purple. Humans weren't the only thing he had slayed, and his soul didn't reek of pain.

"Creag Le Dan Bia," Eugene answered in return.

The beast turned, taking in the way his mouth twisted at the sight of the other rubrum. The light in his chest turned from a soft kind of pink to a dark red. His breathing hitched, and his muscles tightened.

"What did I tell you would happen if I ever saw your worthless hide in my territory again, *boy*?" Eugene blanched, and the beast's brows furrowed.

"That I'd be dog food," Eugene replied. The other rubrum threw his head back and let out a raucous laugh. Behind him, two other demons stepped out of the shadows.

"And yet, you're dumb enough to show your face here again after what you did?" the larger male egged him on, casually crossing the distance between us and them.

"We're just passing through," Eugene said, but his voice lacked conviction. He knew no matter what he said, these assholes weren't leaving. Not with him in one piece. It had me curious to know what happened here, but there were more pressing matters at hand. Like us not dying.

"We?" Creag asked. "You're telling me this lovely specimen is with you?" His eyes turned to us and there was a dark glint, filled with lust and violence. His shirt-less chest puffed up a little bit as he took a step towards us, the bulge in his jeans growing.

Oh hell-to-the-fucking-no.

"You better know how to get us out of this," I told the beast.

"He won't touch us."

Of that, she was completely sure. It did little for my confidence in her when the big ass hell dog turned his eyes to us again. He sniffed the air, and I had a feeling Eugene might become dog chow if we didn't find a way out of here fast.

"Leave her out of this," Eugene spat. At the mention of me, he came forward and tried to put himself between Creag and the beast. She rolled her eyes at the overdra-matic nature of it all.

"I don't think the female is much impressed by you," the purple rubrum mused. "Maybe she needs a real demon to show her a good time—"

"Why is it," the beast began, "that males always think with the head between their legs and not with the one on their shoulders?"

Eugene didn't react, but the other male stiffened. Only when they were feet apart could I tell that the purple rubrum was a good six inches taller. Great.

"Feisty, that one," Creag said. "I like it when they fight back. Makes their flesh taste all the sweeter after they're chained to my bed."

Holy fuck. This dude was nuts. Totally whacko.

I mean, don't get me wrong. Being chained to a bed had my imagination running to all kinds of places...so long as it was with one of my mates.

But this dude got his kicks from violence and torture.

Well, little did he know the beast also liked those things.

Just probably not in the same scenarios he imagined.

"Get out of here, Ruby," Eugene said. His tone was pleading, but he should have known by now that the beast tolerated commands from no one. "Creag, your fight is with me, not—"

"You both talk too much."

The beast whipped her head in the direction where the voice came from.

Moira stepped out of the shadows, her beautiful blue wings tucked in tight behind her. She was dressed in dark leggings and a ripped tank top made to accommodate her new form. Her boots weren't the most practical of choices. They had a three-inch heel, albeit chunky. My best friend's swagger was undeniable, but even the beast could feel her hidden anxiety.

"Getting she-demons to fight your battles for you now, Eugene?" big-ugly said. The beast chafed at his arrogance. She was going to knock him down a foot or three.

"Hey, asshole," Moira called out as she strode forward. She ran a hand through her hair, pulling it back tight so that even in the low lamplight, you could see the mark there. The mark of Cain. "I'm not just any she-demon, fuckface. I'm the devil-damned legion, and you are going to regret messing with the Queen of Hell's errand boy."

Oh no. She did *not* just introduce herself as...fucking hell.

Only Moira would go off touting her new title and mine. Oh, we were going to have words when I got my body back. Me and her, and the beast, and the Horsemen, and even Bandit for good measure, given that the little asshole was growling at the hell monster like he would stand a chance.

Creag Le Dan Bia turned his eyes to her, and what I saw there...it was enough to set the beast off. Envy. Lust. Greed. Violence. He took every inch of my best friend in like she was a feast to be enjoyed.

"Turn and leave now, or your life is forfeit," the beast growled, and it was his only warning.

The large male looked between Moira, the beast, and Eugene, calculating his next move. He lifted his hands in surrender and slowly backed away, one step at a time.

"I hadn't realized who I was dealing with," Creag said.

This rubrum was smarter than Eugene. Maybe that's why he set the beast on edge. Or maybe, it's because she saw a flash of metal as Creag turned to leave. His large arm reached around his back and grasped the handle of what I could only presume was some kind of knife. He twisted as he pulled the blade from its sheath at his back and turned to throw it straight for Eugene—but Eugene beat him to punch.

A dagger protruded from Creag's chest as his skin cracked, very similar to when I killed someone from the inside out using the flames. Except the light appearing in those crevices was not blue, but red. He screamed in anguish, falling to his knees and the dagger stuck in his chest began to glow.

The beast watched, not feeling all that inclined to intervene when his body exploded and ash rained down on them. At the same moment, a flash of red appeared where Eugene was standing, and then he was gone.

"How the fu—"

"Le Dan Bia will be hearing about this," one of the two remaining demons said. He snapped his fingers and the hellhound let out a cry of pain, its collar suddenly extending spikes into its neck. The two henchmen backed into the shadows as the hellhound reluctantly melded into the night. His molten eyes seemed to give off hurt and sorrow, not all that dissimilar to Eugene when we'd first met him.

"You care to explain what the hell just happened?" Moira demanded, crossing her arms over her chest. The beast ignored her question, instead choosing to answer with a question of her own.

"How did you find me?"

"I'm resourceful," Moira replied. The beast was not amused.

"How did you find me?" she repeated.

Moira rolled her eyes. "I'm your familiar and now I'm

a full-blown demon. Seems one of my badass powers is knowing where your ass is at all times."

So, she could track me. That was good to know.

"Why are you here?"

"To join you. Obviously," she answered with the same bored expression and flippant attitude despite the scene before us. The beast eyed her for a moment.

"Are the Horsemen following you?"

Moira grinned savagely. "Why? Do you want them to?"

Her prodding wasn't doing anything for her chances here. Especially when Bandit doubled over on the beast's shoulder, making a deep, choking sound. Seriously...was he laughing? I wondered if he was going to fall off, but he sprawled his body around the back of her neck and sighed his annoyance with her.

After watching Bandit's little display, Moira rolled her eyes again and said, "Doubtful, but possible. Those four have a rather one-track mind, and they are much more concerned with getting you back." This pleased the beast. "Although you wouldn't know it with how shit they are at doing it," Moira muttered at the end.

"I assume you helped them find me at The Devil's Dancers," the beast continued, although most of her attention was focused on the scene before her. A glowing dagger Eugene had thrown. A demon that was killed instantly. A body, and a missing person. But what to make of it?

"Yes, but again, the feckless foursome suck at their job. I ditched them to find you."

The beast nodded. "Do they know you're with me?"

she asked and walked forward to where the knife lay. The blade couldn't have been longer than a foot and the handle was some sort of dark material, covered in glowing red marks and wrapped tightly in place.

"By now? Probably. Without me as their guide, it's doubtful they'll find us anytime soon, though." That was what she wanted to know.

"So, who was the red bloke and why did they want to kill him?" Moira asked, coming to stand beside her as the beast crouched down to better examine the knife.

"His name was Eugene McGee. I don't know why they wished to kill him."

We didn't know, but if Le Dan Bia was after him...

They were the biggest clan on the North American continent. Tasked with maintaining and guarding the portal, they ran this town and everyone in it. Eugene must have pissed them off somehow, but now one of their own was dead, and Moira and I were part of it.

Fuck...

"Do you know where he went?" she asked.

The beast didn't want to answer. No. Not a fucking clue. We didn't know much of anything about this or what went down here tonight, and what we saw...it didn't make sense.

"We should call the Horsemen in," Moira said.

The beast let out a growl. The last thing we needed was them thinking we couldn't handle our own problems. They'd just lock us up again.

"Ruby—"

"I am not Ruby," the beast snarled. She didn't correct Eugene because he needed something to call her. Moira

135

knew better. Our tether, she may be, but that didn't excuse her from the beast's rage.

"Fine. Beast—bitch—cuntmorphon—whatever you want to be called. I say we grab the dagger and—"

Moira reached down and grabbed the handle.

Bandit let out a screech.

Then the world exploded in color.

ALLISTAIR

We were treading on thin ice. In our haste to reclaim her, we lost her again—and this time we didn't have one of her familiars handy to track her down.

No matter. We had someone better.

Sin may not be able to instantly find our girl like a familiar could, but she also wouldn't step out on us at the first failure, and as much as I wanted to flay Rysten for going against the plan—someone had to keep us together. Over four thousand years and we'd never had a true division amongst ourselves. As much as I wanted my mate back, perhaps we needed this.

I glanced over at Julian. The necromancer spoke in a low voice with his back turned, the volatile cold inside of him seeping into New Orleans itself. We needed to find Ruby, but I had to wonder if perhaps my little she-demon wasn't so far gone. Wonder if the beast had known that her leaving would be the thing that would finally spur Julian to make a decision.

He wanted her back as much as the rest of us, if not more.

And in the end, it would make all the difference. We were united now, in our search, our cause, and our reasoning.

Julian hung up the phone and leaned against the granite countertop of the apartment. The beast had trashed a good portion of the first one in her escape. Fortunately, we'd bought the entire building. Relocating to the floor below had only taken a matter of minutes.

"What did she have to say?" I asked him, angling the glass of scotch in my hand. It refracted a face behind me as a woman stepped out of nothing.

She smiled at me in the reflection.

"Hello, Sinumpa," I said cordially.

We had a complicated history. Made more so by her mother. As some of the longest living immortals in both worlds, you ended up running into each other once every hundred years or so.

"Long time no see, Allistair," she replied with a Cheshire smile. Her white hair swayed gently in the air conditioning. The ends were still purple, much like the last time I'd seen her.

"I much prefer this look on you," I said. Our banter always came easily, even if seeing her was anything but.

"Last I saw, you had your eyes on the child you're supposed to be protecting." Her voice lashed at me like a whip, but it missed its mark.

"Ruby is not a child. She's your Queen." Her smirk didn't falter at my reply as she wiggled an eyebrow.

"When you've lived as long as us, most things in the world are children. *Your mate* will only live to be the true Queen if she survives the Six Sins. You should know that."

So, she did know Ruby and I were at least partially mated. Good. That would make this easier, although I didn't appreciate her reminder about the Sins because I was painfully aware of it already. It was yet another reason to make sure her bonds with each of us were cemented before we arrived in Hell. Without them, the Sins might actually break her.

"That's why we need your assistance," Julian broke in. Impatient. He paced back and forth, his hands clenching and unclenching. I knew that Sin saw this in a matter of moments by the way her grin turned vicious.

He was unhinged, and that provided her with an opportunity.

She always was her mother's daughter.

"What you need is enough magic to bind and contain the most powerful she-demon to ever transition. Do not attempt to insult or lowball me, Death. The cost for this will be steep."

I knew what he was going to say before the words left his mouth. It was the only reason I had held off on telling any of them, especially him, that I already knew she was in town. A tangle with Sin was never cheap, and one never came away unscathed.

"Anything for her. I'll pay it."

I looked away. It was never good when you let another immortal know the single piece to use against you, and Julian was making no attempt to hide it in his desperation. He wanted our girl back.

We all did.

And that's why none of us stopped him.

"Excellent. Let's get started."

CHAPTER 11

THE AIR SUCKED IN AROUND US AND POPPED LIKE A bubble.

Where before there had been only darkness, night, and the red glow, now there was only light. Brilliant. Blinding. It filled her vision so fully that there was no darkness. No shadow. No Moira. Only her and the all-consuming power that couldn't simply be described as light. It tasted of wild magic. It smelled like heavy perfume and rain. It brushed over her skin, searching for something.

And then it dissipated. Breaking apart in a shower of sparks, the image shattered, revealing just where she was.

It was a room of some kind, but her vision was disoriented. Off. After seeing only what I could describe as true white, this shroud of darkness was hard to make out. Candles littered the room. From the chandelier above her, to the side tables across the room, to the ones sitting on top of a stack of books, all the way to the ones dotting the circle drawn on the floor below her. Beside her, Moira was sprawled out and moaning. Her eyes were squeezed shut and her brows furrowed. Pain. She was in a lot of pain.

Bandit scrambled to his feet, very much alert as the beast turned to the two figures.

"What is this?" she snarled, her gaze narrowing on Eugene McGee as he stood beside a tall, grey-skinned male with obsidian hair that changed colors like oil in the light. He wore dark fighting leathers, making the silver of his eyes and red glowing brand stand out.

Wait a minute—*shit.*

The blazing red marks on his forehead weren't brands. They were runes.

The etchings on the knife were runes.

Devil-fucking-damnit.

The beast growled under her breath.

This guy wasn't a demon, and fucking Eugene McGee—what had just happened? Red blotted out all reason within her as she let out a roar, breathing fire in an attempt to set the Fae man aflame from across the room. Blue flames spewed from her mouth and ran into an invisible barrier, flattening against it in a wall of black and blue.

Her mouth snapped shut sharply. This was bad. Very bad.

Maybe Moira was right that we should have gone to the Horsemen—

"*No,*" the beast growled at me.

"Are you done now?" the Seelie asked with an air of

annoyance. His accent was foreign, but I couldn't place it.

"Why have you brought me here?" the beast demanded, keeping her eyes on the Fae.

"I didn't bring you anywhere, *child*," the Seelie said distastefully. "*Your* familiar grabbed a weapon that did not belong to her. She's lucky that Gene told me you were not the ones to attack him, or *her* life would have been forfeit."

"You're working with demon hunters," the beast said to Eugene. An almost sheepish blush crept across his cheeks for the second time that night.

"I'm sorry, Ruby. I should have warned you about—"

"The thing inside that girl does not want explanations, my dear." He reached out and rested a hand on the rubrum's shoulder almost affectionately. "And you," he turned back to the beast. "It is unwise to make assumptions on things you know so little about, daughter of Hell."

She narrowed her eyes at him, not liking his tone, or the fact that he knew who we were.

"Oh yes, I know who you are, girl. Most of New Orleans does after the way you've been parading about, mid-transition, leaking ancient magic into the world." I wanted to cop a snide remark at the beast, but it really wasn't the time for that. She was already raging. "*But,* as much as it pains me, I mean you no harm. You healed my lover from his wounds and stood your ground with Le Dan Bia."

"And the binding?" the beast said pointedly, motioning to the red line surrounding her and Moira.

"A necessary precaution for any who try to steal a Fae blade. It's one of the few things in this world that can kill a demon outright. Can't have it go missing, now can I?" he said rhetorically. Still, he didn't drop the barrier.

"I wasn't trying to steal it," Moira rasped from the dirty concrete floor. She sucked in a noisy breath and sat up to cough hoarsely.

Somehow, the blade that brought us here had gone missing after Moira grabbed it and was left sprawled out without an explanation. I didn't trust the Seelie, whether Eugene did or not. But I did respect his power.

"Yes, well, I didn't know that until Eugene took the time to explain it, just before I let the air within the binding crush you." He said it without remorse, much as the beast would have. It was a certain kind of jadedness and I wondered how someone like him could be with someone as naïve as Eugene.

"Enough," the beast commanded. "You know who we are. Now release us."

"Well, you see, I can't do that just yet..." the Seelie trailed off at the deadly glare the beast gave him.

"Donnach," Eugene groaned. "Please don't do this. This isn't her fight."

"Someone has to deal with them, Gene. If not her, then who? Who else has the power to do that outside my own people?" Donnach replied with an undercurrent of anger. Eugene deflated, running a hand over his smooth, bald head.

"I don't like this," the rubrum said.

Donnach's features softened for a fraction of a moment.

"I know, but you know better than anyone what they will do to Morvaen if she remains. I cannot allow that, and she is the only way to prevent a war."

Both Donnach the Seelie and Eugene the rubrum turned to watch the beast. She had one arm tucked under her breast and the other sitting on top of it, bent at the elbow so that she could stroke her bottom lip with the pad of her thumb. Bandit had gone silent during this exchange, as if he could sense the significance of what was happening. Moira had stopped coughing and rose to her feet on wobbly knees, but was very proudly holding her head high and wings partway open.

The Fae sighed, and then he began.

"Know that if I had another option, I would go with it before asking your kind for anything."

If that was meant to make this better, he fell short.

Moira rolled her eyes at him. "Get on with it."

He smiled thinly, razor sharp to the edge of cruelty... but there was something else. Something *old...* This Seelie looked fairly young. Certainly no older than his mid-thirties, and yet...something didn't feel quite right. His eyes spoke of battles gone by. Of bloodshed and brutality.

There was more to him than her eyes were seeing.

"Very well"—he paused to take a breath—"several of my kind are trapped in an underground fighting ring hosted by Le Dan Bia. I'm assuming you know who they are?"

"We care not," came the beast's reply.

The Fae man gave her a withering look.

"You're supposed to be the next Queen, and you

don't care that your people have overstepped their bounds on the planet *my kind* were sentenced to?" he spoke quietly, but his question was bold.

"That was before my time," the beast replied. She shrugged her shoulders and reached around to pet Bandit.

"Yet, you are the heir now."

They stared at each other for a solid minute, neither wanting to crack or yield in any way.

"We did not agree to this. You transported us here against our will, and now you try to manipulate me into solving your problems for you. Find someone else," the beast declared.

Internally I blanched, but the beast watched him without a single fuck to give. They weren't hers. Why would she care?

I sighed. I shouldn't care. I really shouldn't...but I shuddered to think of the fighting rings I had heard of growing up. Of the fighting ring Moira had been subjected to as a child before she was transferred to Portland.

When she'd arrived, her body was bruised and broken. There was a wicked cut on her head that had been haphazardly sewn together. She walked with a limp for six months, and that was after she was able to walk again.

She was a child, barely able to protect herself, and our own kind had thought to use her as entertainment. To beat and break her. She was a demon and they did that to her. What would they do to non-demons? To Fae? To Seelie?

"*It doesn't matter,*" the beast said.

"*It does. If we stand around and do nothing, we are no better than them.*"

"*Save your feelings for our mates. We're not doing it.*"

She was trying to shut me down. Outwardly, the beast turned a quarter of an inch to glance at Moira out of the corner of her eye. My best friend was quiet, and awfully pale. She still remembered those dark times.

The beast was fire and flame, but the wrath that filled me was sharp. Crackling.

I should have let the beast continue fighting and try to rip him to shreds, but I couldn't let this go. Not yet. Not when the anger I felt with her was beginning to break through the carefully structured wall that kept me at bay and her in charge.

"*This is not our problem,*" the beast snarled. "*We don't negotiate with terrorists.*"

Did she really just say that?

"*You don't even know what that means! We're supposed to rule these people. This is every bit our problem,*" I snapped back.

"Why us? Why not him?" the beast finally said through gritted teeth. She was struggling to contain me when I wasn't willing to go along with her plans so easily.

"Eugene used to belong to Le Dan Bia and will be killed on sight—as you saw—before they allow him to step inside their territory. You two, however"—he motioned between the beast and Moira—"they would not realize the danger until it was too late. While young and untrained, you are pure of soul with nearly limitless potential." He walked forward, cocking his head to the

147

side while he watched them both. While clearly shaken, Moira stared back at him with an inner strength that spoke volumes of her person.

"You want us to enter Le Dan Bia's territory, infiltrate their bait ring, and release members of *your* people— putting both of ourselves at risk, for what? So that you don't have to do the dirty work?" Moira spat the words like poison, her anger harsh and cold.

"That's not what I said," the Seelie responded, clearly growing more impatient by the moment. "Any demon can enter their territory without suspicion because they are the portal keepers. Getting into the 'bait ring,' as you call it, would take little effort. I would portal you out of here, directly on their doorstep. The reason I am coming to you"—he motioned to the beast—"is because if I send my people in there, it will result in an all-out war that very well may spread beyond New Orleans. As a new ruler, that is not what I imagine you would want."

That bastard.

He knew what buttons to press and where. The beast, she didn't give many fucks about much of anything. Our familiars? Yes. Our mates? Also, yes. Past that, there were only two things she cared about. One: my safety— we shared a body, so that was a given. The second was our crown.

And a war that spread beyond New Orleans? That most certainly was an issue for the latter.

"We have no reason to trust you," Moira countered. She wasn't wrong, and the beast agreed with her. I did too, for that matter, but apparently, I was the only one seeing reason here, or at least trying to.

Donnach clicked his tongue in annoyance. "She is a young queen asserting herself to her people while doing me a favor," he said sharply. "It prevents a war *this time*, one that I don't think she would like to start her rule fighting. Not while she has many enemies within your own kind. While you may not have a reason to trust me, she also doesn't have one to distrust me. Have I attempted to harm either of you, or the creature, even once?"

The beast glanced at Bandit who stood tall on her shoulder, his teeth bared at the Seelie. His eyes, once black, were now blue like mine and the swirling pentagrams turned like smoke within them—the same as Moira. I'd done it on accident, but like Moira, he remained altered somehow in ways I still hadn't figured out.

"Is declining your offer an option?" the beast asked bluntly.

"I will not take away your ability to choose." He narrowed his eyes. "If you wish to do nothing, I would let you leave and that would be it. However, we will not leave them there to be ripped apart by the beasts of Hell." His voice sounded sincere, but cold. I wished that I could think him a liar. It would have made the situation easier. I wouldn't have felt like they were my responsibility. Like it was me who should fix this. After all, I'd only just stepped into this role. It's not like I was raised to do this.

But I was born to. And the moment Lucifer died, everything began to unravel.

My life. My identity. My powers. The future of not only earth, but Hell itself.

They would continue to unravel until I pulled my big girl panties up and stopped being a pussy.

I wasn't a defenseless half-breed. I could take on demons three times my size. I could escape all four of the Horsemen and outwit them when needed. I had Bandit and Moira at my side, and the beast containing the deadly power inside me. She'd said she was evil's executioner. Maybe she should live up to it.

"I don't trust this," the beast told me.

"You don't have to. But clearly if he can bind us then he could probably do a lot more. He's not wrong about Le Dan Bia. They're a problem, and our names are already on the list thanks to Moira."

The beast stood immobile for what seemed like hours as she considered what to do, but it was really only minutes. Like me, she was coming to the conclusion that we should do this, or at least that we should consider doing this. The Seelie wasn't wrong that by knowingly letting them go after the clan to free their own, we were risking war. As a newly appointed ruler with powerful enemies and a wide opposition, that really wasn't something we could afford. The beast didn't care for politics, but in this she could at least see a glimmer of reason.

We may have left looking for a good time, but it seemed that trouble was always fast to find us. A war with the Seelie was not something we could afford, which meant it was time to step up.

She didn't trust this. Not one bit. But I wasn't yielding to her unless she gave me a damn good reason.

"Don't tell me you're seriously considering this," Moira said. "We can find another way to deal with it. We can send the Horsemen. We can—"

"We do not run from threats, Moira."

My best friend stopped and swallowed hard. She took a minute to stare at the wall across the room, her eyes glazing over as she considered her own reasons. Eventually, she said, "You are powerful, and you are right to not run. But you don't know the evil that lives in places like that. I worry about you—about Ruby—if you choose to go down there."

The beast considered this and with a heavy sigh and deep reluctance, she lowered the barrier that kept me in, protecting me from my own magic. The transition of pushing me forward was sudden and violent, but she sat close to the surface, ready to take it back after I said my piece.

Silently, I thanked her.

"I worry too," I said. Moira's head shot up, her eyes blinking rapidly.

"It's you!" she breathed, throwing her arms around me.

"It's always me," I chuckled and hugged her back. "But I can't stay. The beast is in control because I need her to be. At least until my powers are no longer a danger. She's doing this because I want her—I need her to. We can't allow demons like the ones who attacked Eugene to continue. That's not the kind of Queen I want to be, now or ever."

Moira stepped back and took both my hands in hers. She held them tightly and let loose a steady breath.

"I left the Horsemen and came to find you because I was worried she was going to get you killed. Now I know that it's in fact *both* of you playing off of each other's thought processes that leads you to such awful decisions. I honestly don't know what you'd do without me," she said and gripped my hands so tight the skin around her fingers turned pink.

"You don't have to come with me, you know."

"You're even crazier if you think I'm leaving you to face that alone."

I smiled sadly at her as the beast impatiently waited for me to finish up. "I'll be me again before you know it," I whispered, and with that, I settled into the back of my mind. The beast dropped Moira's hands and settled her hands on her hips as she lifted her gaze to the Fae.

"Double cross us and I will kill him myself." She jutted her chin towards Eugene, who swallowed thickly.

"My dear, if I lied, you wouldn't know it until you stood on the other side of the veil." His words were slippery sweet, but truthful. The Seelie raised his hand and the barrier between us lowered until the light coming from the binding fizzled out.

He lifted his slate colored hand across the space. There was a resolution there, in his eyes. A tautness to his face, a pallor to his skin. This Fae called Donnach was ready and would do anything to bring his people home.

Even make a deal with the devil.

JULIAN

We were born to blood magic. Created with the ability to use it sparingly so that we could combine our strengths. So that we could do the job.

But fate had played out in a very different way. Instead of Ruby bonding with us as familiars to protect her, she and the beast chose us as mates. In our place, she picked familiars from two of what should have been the weakest creatures that would ever walk into Hell. Fate threw us another wrench, in that where their bodies were not strong, their will was. The banshee and the raccoon had a fierceness about them that made them as suited for the job as me. They protected her and Ruby fed on that inner strength within them. It bolstered her where we could not and made her stronger than even us.

If my blood wasn't pounding so hard with aggression and rage, I might have been impressed. Instead, it made me desperate.

I could admit it. So much so that I could make a bargain with Sin.

That I could owe her a favor and enter a blood oath just to get Ruby back.

She wanted a mate that would put her first. Someone that wouldn't just protect, but would own her heart and soul. I would show her what kind of mate I could be.

What kind of mate I *would* be.

She provoked me again and again and again.

Now I was going to make sure she couldn't run. Make sure that she was mine.

Even if I had to tie our very souls together to do it.

Sin cut into my skin again and used the blood to trace her markings. Even after so many years, I never understood the magic she used. How she was able to blend two impossible things. I suspected, much like the other Horsemen did. But we were smart enough to keep our mouths shut in our interactions with her.

"Think of her. Focus on her brand."

She cut down my chest, splitting the bone in two. Most could not survive undergoing this kind of sacrifice. But blood magic had a balance. To receive, you must give a worthy offering.

I wished to own my little Morningstar. To remove her will. To enslave her body.

To do so, I had to give that and more.

Sin plunged her hand into my chest cavity and grasped my still beating heart. I did not allow my mental image to stray for even a second as she pulled it free from my chest.

A dark mass formed around the organ in her hand as

the magic accepted its offering. It devoured my heart, attacking the flesh and blood with inky black tendrils. The magic consumed it whole and then shot downward, returning my heart and filling the void in my chest cavity as my skin closed itself back together. Sin's magic was violent and turbulent as it swept through me, searching for the demon I wished to bond with. Searching for the brand.

I knew the moment it found it.

The moment the blood formed her brand on my chest.

Because in that same moment, I felt the beat of her heart as it pulled me toward her. The magic begged me to fulfill its purpose to the point of pain. The breath hissed between my teeth, but I accepted it. I accepted this pain, because the moment I touched her skin, she wouldn't be free of me and the beast would no longer be in charge.

I was taking her through the transition whether she liked it or not, and there wasn't a fucking thing that she could do about it.

CHAPTER 12

HE FLICKED HIS FINGERS AND SPARKS SHOT FROM the tips. The beast eyed the Seelie warily, but he'd dropped the barrier. He'd explained what was to come. He'd sworn on rune magic to do us no harm except in defense, and he hadn't made the beast swear the same.

I wasn't sure if it was stupidity, arrogance, or something else entirely.

I'd never seen someone work so fast. His fingers flew through the motions, as if playing piano in the air. Red, swirly shit appeared everywhere he touched. The glowing marks didn't make much sense to me, but after a few seconds of nothing happening, I felt it.

He stopped, lowering his hands. There was a massive whoosh like we'd stepped into a vacuum and the marks shone brighter, becoming more intense as they moved to converge. The air crackled with power as the magic formed an incandescent orb. The sheer force that radiated from it unsettled the beast. The thing sucked in all the magic from the air, pulling physical objects toward it. A couple of books came flying out of their piles and ended up being absorbed in the damn thing as it nearly tripled in size before exploding outward. A portal six-feet in diameter snapped into place.

On one side stood the beast, Moira, Bandit, Eugene, and the Seelie. On the other, separated only by a thin film of red magic—a dark street leading towards a shadowed alley.

In truth, I didn't understand a lot about how their magic worked. I'd only heard snippets here and there growing up, but to my understanding, runes—or brands as I knew them—held power. Power the Seelie could tap, just as the Unseelie used blood. They were old magic. Older than any demons I knew of, including the Horsemen. I kept those thoughts to myself as the beast walked forward, toeing the edge of the portal.

The entrance to the underground fighting ring.

"If this is a set-up, *harvester,* you will be sorry," the beast warned. Although he had sworn up and down not all Seelie were out to kill our kind, the beast was less forgiving and more irritated with him than I.

"Duly noted, *child,*" he replied, putting just enough sneer into his voice that the beast's fingers twitched with the desire to backhand him.

Without any formal goodbye or even a glance at Eugene, the beast stepped through the portal. For a moment, her movements were sluggish as the magic strained against her skin, simulating the feeling of moving through water. With a pop, it broke, and she crossed over, stepping onto dry pavement. Bandit shook himself like a wet dog and began grooming his paws while the beast waited for Moira.

She didn't take long. Coughing and spluttering, she stumbled through the portal, her right wing smacking into Bandit. He let out a cry of dismay and jumped to the ground. He ran at her and bit her pinky finger, jumping away before she could swat at him.

"Ow! Little asshole, what the fuck is wrong with—"

"Come." The beast leaned over and he hauled himself up onto her shoulder again as she strode into the night. Moira let out a slew of curses behind them but followed after.

Above them, the skies looked tumultuous. Thick clouds blotted out every star, reflecting back the lights of the city in a red haze that lit the midnight streets of New Orleans.

She walked down the broken sidewalk, stepping around the chunks of concrete and smashed beer bottles. She didn't even cringe as the tiny shards of glass cut her feet. In front of her, the alley loomed. Tall. Imposing. With the red haze in the sky, she should have been able to see down it. An umbrella of dark magic and midnight covered it entirely, hiding away what lay below—unless you knew it was there.

Together they made their way forward, stepping through the veiled murkiness. Her foot felt something smooth. Another, but this one was lower. Stairs. They were going down stairs. She continued, taking the lead as they descended further, and the path slimmed. She still couldn't see anything apart from the glow from Moira's wings, but she could feel it. Feel the dark magic around her. Feel Bandit as he clung to her, quietly mewling with displeasure. The beast ran a hand through his fur, soothing him, and my raccoon purred.

At the very bottom, they stopped, and Moira lifted a quivering hand to knock twice. The sound reverberated through her bones, echoing up the stairway.

"Are you certain you can handle this?" the beast asked softly into the dark night.

"Too late to turn back now," Moira grunted. Her heart was hammering so loud even we heard it.

The door swung open, and a tall male zeroed in on Moira, assessing her with interest before turning his predatory eyes on us. The beast stared back without emotion, impassive as always. Time for that moment of truth. Did the Seelie deceive us? Or was it really going to be just that simple?

The yellow-eyed chupacabra stepped back and held the door open, silently letting us pass. From behind him, music thrummed with a steady beat and a mix of alcohol, sweat, and blood wafted in the air, luring the beast into the underground shithole with the promise of violence and booze. Can't say I faulted her thinking as she roughly shoved past him, lightly casting him aside with a push of her hand as he tried to crowd toward her. I doubt he even noticed the exotic pull my body held over him. All the better that she tossed his ass around to snap him out of it. We weren't here for sex. If that's what she wanted, we had four mates just dying to get a location on us.

The beast walked into the bar like a guy with a big dick in the locker room. You know the type. She strutted in as if she owned the place and heads turned.

Behind her, Moira's chest had gone into overdrive. Fear. Anger. Hurt. *Pain.* She wasn't handling this. She wasn't coping. Her distress made the beast hesitate, and Bandit dug his claws into her. Blue blood dripped down her shoulder as a painful clarity cut through her mind, allowing her to separate our emotions and Moira's. Several male demons, imps by the looks of them, decide to try coming up to us. Bandit bared his teeth at them and let out a hiss, even when they switched to approaching Moira who was only just starting to break through her own paralyzing fear.

The beast grabbed her by the wrist and pulled her forward, ignoring the curious onlookers. This was a bad idea. Really, quite awful actually. Why did I think bringing Moira here was a good idea to begin with?

I didn't. I listened to the word of a hunter and let my own judgement be colored by a sob story. I wanted to protect my crown and stand up for what's right. But look where it got us.

The beast shook her head at my doubts and second-guessing. We had come this far, and she was going to do what *we* set out to do.

The concrete flooring was discolored. Stained in shades of brown and blue.

Blood. It was stained with blood.

To her left, the floor dropped off with nothing but a pathetically weak rail to prevent people from going over the edge and into the hell below. Blood and dirt smeared the walls down there and something let out a terrible screech of pain. Bandit instantly began growling. This place even made him nervous. He didn't like being here, so out in the open like. It made him...uneasy.

And all I could think about was that Moira had told us. She'd warned us of the kind of evil that lurks in places like this. In clans like Le Dan Bia.

We didn't want to listen.

But we were here now, and despite the paralyzing fear within her and the anxiety Bandit was now giving off, both her and the beast had every intention of showing them that we won't tolerate this.

The place itself stank of piss and death. How anyone could keep a child down here...yeah, the beast was going to knock some heads in before we left. She wasn't going to be complacent with this kind of behavior. Neither of us would.

She continued towards the bar in the back, well away from the pit and fighting that went on below. She walked right up to it like she wasn't dragging Moira behind her, and slapped her hand on the sticky surface, ignoring the pungent odor around us. The male behind the bar turned as he finished lighting a joint. Instantly, the scent of white lotus hit us, sharpening the need in our core. The beast grimaced, eyes flicking to the burning end as it exploded in his face. He jumped back, moving to drop it, but it had already disintegrated into nothing more than black dust.

His dark eyes flicked from the wasted lump of ash in his hand to our face, growing angrier by the second. Fangs slid into place and he lunged to grab our hand. The beast moved faster. Releasing Moira, she grabbed a half empty beer bottle from the demon standing two feet over —and smashed it on his skull. Stale beer spilled over the shade that thought to hurt her, splattering her own form. Bandit leapt at him, attaching himself with great vigor to the demon's face. He stumbled back, hitting the wall before regaining his senses.

He moved to grab Bandit and she let out a shrill whistle. My raccoon disengaged, tearing one of the barman's eyeballs out as he jumped away. The painful scream rivaled that of the creature in the pit below, and Bandit only barely avoided the swipe of a clawed hand as he landed on the bar in a hissing pile of fur. The beast held out her arm and he climbed up, reaffirming his place as he glared at the now one-eyed demon.

I hoped she knew what she was doing, because the last time we left a one-eyed demon hanging around, he tried to kill me, and almost killed Moira. The beast laughed, cold and callous, as she sent his body up in flames.

The demons around us jumped back, only now realizing the predator that walked in their midst. She held the broken neck of the beer bottle in one hand as a makeshift weapon and a globe of fire in the other.

"*We were supposed to come in under the radar,*" I glowered at her.

"*This place reeks of perversion. They must be taught a lesson.*"

Devil-damnit. Every fucking time I thought she had the right idea going, she turned around and pulled something like this. Every fucking time.

"*You better keep Moira and Bandit safe,*" I snapped at her, not wanting to distract her too much.

"*I always do*," she replied, seemingly unperturbed by my frustration.

Crazy psycho bitch.

She almost grinned at that comment. Of course she would. Only crazy people found it amusing to be called so.

"Who are you, and what are you doing here?" the demon from the door said as he walked to the front of the crowd, no longer as appraising as he'd been.

Good. That will make this easier—wait a minute— was that her thinking? Or was it me?

Oh fucking hell. This whole sharing a body thing was really screwing with me.

"Who I am, matters not. I've come for the Seelie you stole."

"It's her!"

For fuck's sake. Could we not catch a break here?

"That's Lucifer's spawn and the legion."

Moira stiffened and blinked. She lifted her head, and when she looked at them she saw shadows. I didn't need to ask to know what they represented to her. What this place represented to her. I had come to peace with my past, but Moira never had.

She had never needed to, until now.

"Interesting," the chupacabra from the door said. "You kill Creag Le Dan Bia and then return for the hunters. I can't see any daughter of Lucifer being a Seelie sympathizer." The demon looked at her for a long moment, and then he looked to the others in the room. "What do you have to say about that, lads?" It was only then that she noticed the vicious grin on his lips. "Do we have ourselves a fake?"

Several of them regarded the fire she held in one hand, but clearly it didn't scare them enough. She'd taken on demons twice her size the last week when standing up for the weak and abused, but a hundred demons? Maybe more? Even I wasn't sure she could handle that many. That we hadn't grown overconfident in ourselves and only just realized the hole we dug. While some feared the power she held, others seemed completely unperturbed by the fact she'd killed one of their own with little thought.

Savages.

I had thought it, but Moira said it. She spat the word from her mouth like venom and snapped her wings open in all their glory.

"Savages, you say," he mused, smiling with very pointed teeth. "Darling, you haven't seen savage if this scares you." He lifted a hand and snapped his fingers.

Three demons came forward in a bid to grab us and the beast let out a growl.

"Touch her and you're fucking dead."

She stilled.

We knew that voice.

That cold whisper of *Death.*

"Oh thank fuck," Moira breathed.

The beast swung her head around looking for the source, but she saw nothing except unfamiliar faces. Then the brand on our chest began to burn—and I mean *burn.* It sizzled with a sharp all-consuming pain that almost felt like pleasure as it spread throughout her body.

The three demons paused, also looking for the source of the threatening voice—only to come up dry.

They took another three steps toward me before coming to a violent halt. One by one, their skin blackened from the inside out. The whites of their eyes turned blue before exploding.

I'd seen that happen only once before. Most shades were not skilled enough to do that much damage to someone's system. However, Pestilence was not most shades.

He'd killed Josh with as little effort. These three assholes were nothing—and while it likely wouldn't kill them—they wouldn't be able to heal from this kind of damage for hours.

That meant hours writhing in agony.

I rather liked that thought, even if another lance of red hot pain was shooting through our body. The beast blinked, just as confused as I about what was going on— and the next thing I knew, it wasn't her staring out of my eyes—but me.

What in Satan's name—

I didn't even have the time to finish my thoughts before someone grabbed me from behind. To my credit, the beast was not the only one that had some cool moves. Armed with a broken beer neck, I let my adrenaline take over as I twisted to the side and slashed out.

Cold blue ichor hit my face as I severed the demon's carotid artery.

The only problem was that this was not just any demon.

It was Death. He'd found me.

And right now, he looked pissed as hell that I tried to kill him. Again.

All bravery left me as I turned to run—but Julian was smarter than that. He wasn't letting anyone get me out of here this time.

Julian grabbed my hips roughly, slinging me over his shoulder. I didn't even register him moving before we stepped into the shadows and all sounds of the brawl taking place behind me receded.

The beast had wanted to court Death. She liked playing games.

Once again, I somehow got stuck paying the price because the bitch got her wish.

Me.

Him.

And if the sudden change in temperature was any indication, nowhere to go for miles.

** LARAN **

Where were they?

Rysten and Allistair were sweeping the city while I made my way through the underground, but it seemed that every sign of Moira and Bandit was gone. I held out the bag of cookies I'd brought with me, just for the furry creature.

"Bandit! Bandit!" I called his name, shaking the bag. Usually he would come to me instead of the other Horsemen, but this time he was nowhere to be seen. The underground of Le Dan Bia was all but empty apart from me. I let out a frustrated breath and didn't bother wasting my time calling for the banshee. She would start screaming eventually and all of New Orleans would know where to find her, but the raccoon was not as simple.

"Have you found anything?" Allistair's presence brushed against my mind for a moment. Worry edged at him as well.

"Nothing," I answered, leaning against the bar. Most of the demons that had been here were either knocked out cold or dead. Their bodies littered the floor. Fuckers deserved it after trying to harm Ruby and Moira. I'd always hated Le Dan Bia. They were always straining at Satan's leash and out of the seven portal keepers, their clan always had the most reports against them. We'd be doing the world a favor wiping them from existence, but I knew this was far from the whole of the clan. Once some of the ones who weren't dead healed, they would wake and try to come for us with a vengeance. It was the only reason the three of us were wasting our time scouring the city for Moira and Bandit. We needed them out of the equation while Ruby transitioned. Somewhere they would not be in harm's way. That was difficult to do when you can't find them.

Still, I kept searching and I would continue until I found them.

We just had to hope for our sake—and Ruby's—that it wasn't too late when I did.

CHAPTER 13

Trees, dirt, and the sound of howling wind told me we weren't in New Orleans proper anymore. The ground below was dark, too dark to make out much beyond the forest floor. Leaves crunched as he began walking, not stopping to put me down. His breathing was quick, harsh.

"Hey! What are you doing—" I snapped, kicking at him. He reached up and swatted my ass. Another flare of pain ignited in my chest where my brand pulsed. My hips bucked against his hand—that he hadn't removed. He squeezed tightly through the little black number I wore, a growl starting deep in his chest. I smacked my hands against his own backside, my interest perking up at the hard muscle I found there. Once again, the strength I could sometimes display was gone—leaving me weak to Julian's manhandling.

"I would not keep fighting me if I were you, Ruby," he said quietly.

It was only then that I homed in on the dangerous emotions swirling in his chest. They were no longer closed off like the last time I saw him when the beast handily took out the four of them. Now he was wide open, a mix of anger and fear and a need so sharp it was painful.

I'd known he was jealous because he wanted me as the others did, but I'd never realized how much. Just how deep it ran.

I'd once said if he wanted a woman that not even Heaven or Hell could separate them. Little did I know then how true that was.

"What are you going to do to me, Julian?" I asked, my voice more than a little unsteady. I blamed it on the blood running to my head from being held upside down this long.

"What do you think I should do to you, Ruby?" he asked in return.

Devil fuck me. The things his voice did to me. Another spasm of pain ran through me, straight to the apex of my thighs. I let out a desperate mewling sound and Julian stiffened. His hand trailed over the back of my thighs, singeing my sensitive skin with fire. I squirmed, trying to get out of his hold, but he held tight, never giving me an inch.

"Stop fucking with me, Julian. You're being an ass," I snapped in a heated frustration. A sharp jolt went through me as his hand came down hard on my ass.

Did he just spank me...?

"Yes, I did. And I'm going to do a lot more than that if you keep testing me."

There we go again with that nifty mind-speak thing, except he could hear mine apparently. I grumbled under my breath and deflated a little bit. His hand flattened against me, gently rubbing over my now blazing ass.

I wanted to send another string of curses at him, but this felt good. In a strange, fucked-up kind of way. Pain can be pleasure after all, if administered correctly. He slipped his fingers just beneath my dress, into the thin panties. I squirmed again, not quite comfortable with how intimate this felt given I couldn't see him or move. His fingers expertly slid over one cheek and down the center, entering my heated skin.

"Do you know how you smell to me?" Julian asked quietly.

He slipped two fingers into my wet folds, pressing down to hit my G-spot as he pushed them in and out. I let out a low moan, turned on so much by his aggressive nature. He could be as cold as he fucking wanted as long as his fingers kept doing what they were doing.

"Did you know that your very scent changed the night the beast came forward because you had subconsciously chosen me as a potential mate?"

No. I didn't know that, but I also didn't really care. He pressed down, rubbing in circles. Slow. He was going excruciatingly slow.

What the hell was wrong with him?

Fire lanced through me, very real this time as my frustration grew. I smiled wickedly at the smell of burning cloth.

Julian removed his fingers and slapped my ass.

"Don't fucking try it."

I growled at him and slapped his ass back. It's not like I could fucking control it. I was in the middle of the transition and he was fucking playing with me, going on about how I smell when I just wanted him to fuck me.

"You'll be fucked when I decide to fuck you," Julian snapped.

What the–

Did I say that out loud?

"No, but your mind is wide open—and before you think it—no, I don't give a shit that you can't control it either."

Ass.

That got me another slap on my backside.

Bastard. I arched my back and brought my elbow up and around, contacting with the back of his skull. Julian let out a groan, his grip slipping, and I swiftly kicked him in the jewels.

Had these fuckers learned nothing? The beast and I shook our heads in annoyance as breath whooshed from his lips. I toppled sideways, my back hitting the hard ground beneath me. I groaned as sticks punctured my skin uncomfortably, and then jumped to my feet.

I took off into the trees without waiting to see him follow. Part of me knew I wouldn't get very far. It was pitch black outside. The entire place was nothing but shadow—which meant this was his element. Still, the rest of me was annoyed with him for this manhandling bullshit. He could have just taken me how I wanted, but instead he throws me over his shoulder and acts like an asshat. I wasn't inclined to make a single part of this easy for him after the last week.

I ran blindly into the woods, not daring to look behind even as he shouted at me.

"You do not want to play this game with me, Ruby! It's only going to make it worse when I do get you. You played with Death, and it's time to pay up."

Too late, motherfucker. You should have thought about that before—

Agh!

My feet snagged on a root sending me face first into the forest floor.

"Devil-damned—motherfucking—cunt-kissing—asshole—" My string of curses was cut off sharply by my body being flipped over against my will.

I stared up at Julian's pale form standing over me. Even in the dark I could see his eyes blazing with fury.

"I told you not to run," he glowered.

I stared back, all smartass retorts drying up on my tongue. He was shirtless—why was he shirtless? Didn't he know that a girl can't think straight with all those perfectly defined abs just waiting to be licked—

A smirk tugged at his lips.

Shit! I was doing that mind thing again. I just knew it. Julian held out his hand for me to take it. Part of me wanted to, but the rest of me knew not to be swayed but such a simple gesture. His rage and desire were eating him alive from the inside out, bleeding into me.

I slapped his hand away and moved to stand, only to find myself lifted and my back slammed against a tree. I gasped, trying to feel my way up from down. I only knew it was a tree because of the rough bark scraping at my back. Julian was gripping my hips way

173

tighter than necessary, and there was no getting out of it this time.

"Wrap your legs around my waist," he commanded.

"Fuck you," I spat.

Did I really mean that? I don't know. His emotions were out of control, which was sending mine out of control.

"Ruby, do not fucking push me right now—"

And what do I do?

I slap him.

Full on bitch-slap to the face, and apparently my seriously not reliable super-strength had come back because his face whipped around as the crack echoed into the night.

Whatever burning fury he felt before was nothing to what would come next.

Slowly, so slowly that my anxiety inched up another ten notches, he turned his head back toward me and I saw it: the awful turbulence of emotions in his eyes. The emotions that he didn't know how to hide from me any longer. Just as I couldn't seem to keep my thoughts from him.

I sensed it in him. The shift. So sudden and swift. He lowered one hand to my bare thigh, hoisting it up around his waist, followed by the other. His cock twitched against me as he rubbed me through the thin material of my panties with the hard friction of his jeans. Even though it went against everything inside of me, I moaned, my back arching off the tree as the desire clashed hot and hard against the burning anger inside me.

"Do you hate me?"

I don't know what possessed me to say it. Probably the tornado of emotions running through me, angry and unforgiving. That's how it felt inside.

But his—his felt like a volcano, the pressure boiling and just waiting to erupt.

Still, the moment the words left my lips, Julian paused and the look he gave me...it was broken. So broken.

And that's when I knew.

"I wish I did. It would make my job so much easier," he whispered. His breath was cool as the arctic when it fanned my face. He reached up and brushed a stray lock of blue hair away from my face. "I can't hate you, Ruby. Not even when you—" He broke off, swallowing hard. There it was again, that vulnerability he covered with fury. "Not even when you ran from us. You let the beast in, and you ran from us. We had no idea where you were. We couldn't find you—and when we did, you were with that—that *male*." His voice came to a stop, his eyes darkening once more and it all made sense. He slipped his hand down the side of my face, his fingers applying pressure to my throat as he held me there.

"You think I..." I paused, watching the anger in his gaze fizzle up again like a darkness he couldn't shake. "I healed Eugene's soul. That is why he was with me. You should know by now that I'm not interested in anyone else, Julian." My voice was soft. A reprimand, but gentle. Kind, if not for the slight growl at the end. The beast wanted to throttle him for being a territorial idiot.

His hold on my throat loosened as he swept his thumb across my jawline almost...tenderly.

175

"You can't see him again," Julian insisted. Completely irrational, as always.

"You can't tell me who I can and can't see," I replied.

I didn't care to see him again, but it was the principle. They needed to learn this and learn it now. I was not taking orders from them. If we were equals, then damnit, they needed to treat me like it.

Julian dropped his hand from my throat, sliding it down to rest over my chest.

"I don't like other males near you."

Really, Sherlock? I couldn't have guessed. Julian's lips thinned as he stared at me. Yeah, he heard it. I didn't give a shit.

"Eugene is gay, Julian. You're being unreasonable."

He blinked. "I still don't like it."

I brought my hand up to smack myself in the forehead. Were we really doing this?

"I don't like a lot of things, but you don't see me being a dick about it. Maybe instead of being an ass, you should give me a reason to stick around and not feel the need to leave, then I won't be running into other demons."

Julian seemed to consider this before he asked, "What kind of reason?"

He leaned forward, his breath grazed just below my ear, sending a wave of chills over me. I groaned. His lips pressed against my throat as he brushed them up and down.

"What kind of reason, Ruby?"

Oh fucking hell. His mood swings were giving me whiplash.

"You could stop being a jealous prick and make a move if you want to be with me."

Why had I just phrased it that way? Great mood killer, Ruby. You and your socially awkward mouth.

"And spanking my ass doesn't count," I added.

Julian didn't even seem perturbed by me calling him on it. On the other hand, he seemed a lot more at ease once I cleared away his fears of Eugene—although I wasn't apologizing for running. Not over my dead body.

"I rather like spanking your ass," he replied, his erection digging into me.

He slid his hand back to my throat and tightened it. It wasn't enough to choke, but the possessiveness that lay beneath it was clear.

And you know what? I liked it.

In fact, I kind of loved it.

But I wasn't letting him off that easy.

"And I like not being treated like a child."

For some reason, I felt like I needed to push this because as soon as the clothes came off, I would be a goner. And they were coming off. Very soon. That much I was sure of.

Another lance of pain slashed through my chest, stronger this time. Fire tore through the forest as I cried out in an excruciating pain that was tinged with the briefest of pleasures.

I didn't understand what was going on. I'd gone days in transition without this happening. What had changed? What had—

Guilt.

It bled through from the only other living creature

around me as Julian held me tighter, rocking his hips into mine. The contact made it better, more bearable, even as the fire grew out of control and began to incinerate our clothes.

If I thought I was out of control before, that was nothing compared to this.

"What did you do?" I moaned, knowing that he was somehow at fault. Julian swallowed hard as he ran his hands up and down my bare flesh. It made the pain better, but this time it wasn't completely abating.

"I'm...I'm sorry, Ruby. I didn't know what to do—" his voice broke off as a scream built in my chest. His touch helped, but it wasn't enough. Whatever he had done was making the transition a thousand times worse.

I thrashed against him as images filled my mind. Images of him and the others. Images of blood being spilled. Images and snapshots of what he did.

That fucker.

He'd *bound* me. Truly bound me. Except he didn't bind me in a circle. Oh no, he didn't have the power for that once I had left, so he did the next best thing.

He bound me to *him*. As long as I was in the transition, my body needed his. Begging for his touch to the point of pain if I didn't fulfill it.

He wanted to make sure I didn't run again, and he bound us together so that I couldn't.

"You motherfucking, cock-sucking, son of a—"

His mouth descended on mine, hard and insistent. I stayed frozen to the spot at first, not wanting to give in despite what my body and heart so desperately desired, but that's the thing about this bond. It made him a drug to me—

The thought was snatched away before I could see it and I growled at him. Julian knew that he couldn't hide now. Not after what he'd done.

I leaned into him, wrapping my arms around his neck. I clasped my hands flat over the back of his neck, pulling him to me before I dove into his mind.

His kiss turned rough—savage—as he pushed me back into the already burning tree. Our clothes were all but ash at this point, and his bare erection was hard against my skin as it slid over me without entering.

He groaned, his nails biting into my thighs as I nipped at his bottom lip.

"What's the rest of it, Julian?" I asked breathlessly, slipping a hand to cup his jaw, leaving the other on the back of his neck. "There was more to what you did, and you took the memory away before I could see it. What are you still trying to keep from me?"

Ignoring me, he sank his teeth into my shoulder, and it wasn't just an act of passion. He wanted to mark me. To make me his. He trailed his lips up my jaw and down my throat.

"What did you fucking do, Julian?" I asked one last time.

I really didn't want to test how well I could go through his mind. It felt like an invasion of privacy, but if he wouldn't tell me, I would do it. After all, he was the one who took my choice away and used fucking blood magic to bind my body to his. Not that I didn't want it

KEL CARPENTER

long before he did so, but the act itself was still dancing on the hairsbreadth edge of right and wrong.

Julian growled as I fisted his hair and writhed against him. He rocked into me as kama started pouring out from him. It filled the air around me and I breathed it in, relishing the crisp cut that tore through my throbbing core.

Damn him, he was addictive.

The tree behind me cracked and I began to topple backwards as the massive oak no longer supported our weight, but instead of hitting the forest floor, my back hit something soft and I could feel the smooth sheets and comforter beneath me.

The room was black as pitch and my flames had stopped burning at some point. I moved to pull back, but Julian gripped me tightly, biting into my other shoulder.

"What the fuck—"

My body shuddered as his hardness rubbed against the sensitive bundle of nerves that left me moaning. There was pleasure in pain if done right. Wasn't that what I always had said?

How right I was.

"We had to find you, so I did the only thing I could do," he whispered against my neck and then the scene opened up again.

He knelt in a dark room, and a girl—a girl I recognized—stood before him. Her white blonde hair barely shifted as she leaned forward and cut his skin. Then she used his blood to draw the runes. The runes that would pull me to him.

So that I would feel what he feels. So that once he

touched me, I would crave him for the remainder of the transition. So that I couldn't run. Even if I left this planet, he would find me. He would always find me.

But the blood magic wasn't so simple as to give him everything with nothing in return.

To form the bond, all barriers between us would become non-existent. I would feel what he feels...and in return, he would endure my pain should I run or resist.

The intense burning that filled my chest also filled his. The pain he felt was now mine.

He'd all but chained me to him, and in doing so, chained himself to me too.

All to keep me safe...well, not quite, but mostly. His desires were thick and raw and filled with such sweet agony. He wanted to do things to me, things he tried to protect me from.

None of the Horsemen were good men, Julian especially, and I'd broken whatever control he had when I left them.

The worry ate at him. The fury clawed. It shattered all pretenses that he held that kept him from crawling to my bed and led him to making a bargain with the girl who could do blood magic.

To get me and to keep me, he all but opened his soul.

I should be furious. I should fight him, and the beast, with every ounce of my being because of the kind of male Julian was. Because the type of possessive behaviors I'd run from my whole life ran deep in him.

But he wasn't just Death.

He was Julian.

My Julian. The one who would do anything to

protect me, even come to terms with himself and the truth he already knew.

I was his greatest weakness, and yet, staying away from me—even *for* me—was never an option. The beast and I chose him as a mate and he accepted it. I was his, in every sense of the word.

But he was also mine, and that kind of surrender didn't come naturally to Death. He forced my hand, but in doing so, he finally made up his goddamn mind.

Was it strange that I was almost happy he had done this? Desire may be its own demon that demands you feed it, but so was love—even the twisted kind. I wondered if this was a bit of both because he and I were finally on the same page.

I ran my fingers through his hair and it was softer than I expected. I tugged his head so that I could pull him up and he acquiesced, resettling his weight by moving both arms above my head.

"I understand," I whispered.

He stared down, his eyes so dark they didn't even look green. I wanted to say more, but another pain lanced through my chest. This one worse than the others before. I let out an awful throat-straining scream. My back arched off the bed as I simultaneously tried to get closer to him and crawl out of my skin. I understood why he had done it, but the pain he put me in—the pain he put us both in—was immeasurable. I don't know how he was bearing it without cringing. Tears blotted the corners of my eyes as my body twisted, trying to break away from the torment even though I knew I couldn't.

"Make it stop," I begged. "Please make it stop."

There was only one way it would. He and I both knew that now.

Julian pulled back off the bed causing it to worsen. I clawed at my chest and he snatched my hands, pulling them away.

"Sit and don't move," he commanded.

I did as I was told, sitting on the edge of the bed. He released my hands and knocked my legs apart with his knee. I trembled with anticipation, widening my legs without needing further instruction as he kneeled in front of me. He leaned forward and softly kissed the brand between my breasts, the bone-splintering pain lessening, dulling. I brought my hands around to rest on his shoulders. Contact was helping.

His lips trailed down my naked chest, over my abdomen, straight to the aching heat between my legs. He grasped one of my thighs and pulled it over his shoulder, lightly blowing on my clit. A ragged gasp escaped my lips as he leaned forward and continued blowing as he buried two fingers inside me. I rubbed my hands over his shoulders and down his back, scratching him with my nails. He growled against me and my hips surged forward, but he held me still as he ran his tongue over me.

The oddest sensation filled me as the beast internally guided my hands to the back of his neck. A burning sensation rippled through me, and once again, I was too late to realize it was happening. Julian knew, and he stopped as the fire burned between us.

Where I should have been crying out in release, I nearly sobbed in desperation as I branded him. I was so fucking close when the burning receded, but a small part of me had the good sense to not scream at him. He was going to fuck me, of that I was certain.

"You branded me," he murmured.

Was that awe in his voice? Couldn't be...I tried to write it off, but it wasn't so easy when his emotions flooded me.

"Don't act so surprised," I snapped, not nearly as apologetic as I'd been when it happened with Laran or Allistair. Julian bound me without asking. He was already in this for life. His ass didn't get an apology. He laughed, pulling away.

"What are you doing?" I groaned, spreading my legs wider to show just how desperate I was.

"Turn around and get on your hands and knees," he ordered.

Whereas Laran and I had been interrupted, Julian had every intention of fucking me sore before the other Horsemen caught up to us. Wherever we were. That was a different question for after I came.

I pulled back onto the bed and did as he told me. The bed dipped as Julian got on behind me. He lifted the hair from my neck and pulled it taut.

"Lift yourself up. I want to feel you," his voice rumbled huskily.

My stomach muscles contracted as I pulled myself up, my back coming flush against his chest. He wrapped an arm around my waist, placing his hand over my stomach. I pushed my ass back, trying to rub against him. Clearly it wasn't as alluring as I thought when he let out a dark chuckle.

"What do you want, Ruby?" he asked, his voice no more than a whisper in my ear.

"You know what I want, asshole," I growled.

My breath hissed between my teeth as I felt a sharp smack on my sex. It stung, but this kind of pain felt good.

"You're being a brat. We'll need to work on that."

I shivered against his words, but not in fear. He may have been more savage when it came to pleasure, but I felt nothing but safe with him. So, I kept my mouth shut this time.

"Much better." I could hear the grin in his voice. "Now, what do you want?"

The pain in my chest ripped through me, shredding through any snarky retorts I had left.

"You!" I screamed.

Julian growled in approval and then he released me. My shaking limbs were barely holding me with all the tension coiled in my muscles. The lightest tap on my back was all it took for me to fall forward, landing on my elbows, face down. My legs shook with anticipation as his head touched my entrance. He thrust once, filling me in one go. I moaned into the sheets as I fisted them, biting down on the smooth fabric as my body nearly came apart.

What in Satan's name—how big was he? It's not like I was a virgin, but damn. I hadn't been fucked in years. May as well be. Still, when he pulled out, that familiar heat flared in me, still so close to the edge. He slammed back into me and I rocked forward.

I barely registered my hair being lifted as Julian wound it around his palm. He gripped it, pulling it taut, wrapping his arm around my torso, guiding my body up so that I was right where he wanted me.

And he thrust into me. Again, and again, and again.

With my back arched and his hand splayed across my abdomen, I lost myself to sensation as he pounded into me. I didn't even feel the climax creeping up before it tore through my system, making me clamp around him as I shuddered with relief and screamed his name.

He liked this. I could sense it as he continued to pump into me, chasing his own release. I pulled on the kama around me, inhaling deep breaths as I pushed my ass back, giving myself to him wholly. He thrust into me once more and roared. The wood panels above us shook under the force of his power. I thought he was going to level the house.

When the trembling stopped, and our breathing calmed, he let go of me. I fell forward on weak knees.

"You can't possibly think I'm done with you yet," his breath whispered over me.

The beast purred, and she wasn't the only one.

It was going to be a long night.

CHAPTER 14

I STARTED TO FALL INTO A BLANKETED HAZE OF LUST and kama.

I don't know how long had passed or how many times he had taken me before I noticed the eyes watching us. The golden gaze that prowled from the corner of the room. Allistair stepped out of the shadows and the crisp cut of winter was joined by something sickly smooth as honey. It wrapped around my limbs, holding me in place while Julian fucked me from behind.

Not that I would have been able to move anyway with my face pressed into the mattress and him holding my arms behind my back. Julian had more of a fetish than Allistair when it came down to not letting me move. Demons and their kicks.

I felt it the moment Julian noticed who'd walked in on us. The slightly possessive tinge to him as he pounded me relentlessly. One hand held my wrists and the other gripped my hip, guiding me into him how he saw fit.

Allistair stood on the sidelines, his body relaxed, his gaze anything but.

Let it be known, I had never considered myself an exhibitionist. Until the transition, I'd never taken to watching others or letting them watch me. There was something so raw, but so intimate about it. Me watching him, while he watched Julian take me.

His hands moved to slip off his suit jacket, leaving it on the floor where he stood. My heart quickened.

Was he going to join us?

"Would you like me to join you?" he asked aloud.

I felt behind me, waiting for the intense jealousy that filled Julian before. While I was in no way his exclusively, I was theirs, and I needed to consider how they felt.

The beast reached forward tentatively, pushing me to encourage Allistair. While the blood magic Julian had done prevented her from coming forward until this was over, she was very much still there.

And she very much wanted him too.

Julian released his grip on my wrists, my arms falling to my sides, his hand reaching down and pressing against my hardened nub. He pinched the pinnacle nerve bundle, drawing a low moan from my lips. Golden particles wet my tongue, inciting another bout of sex driven cravings. I couldn't get enough of this stuff. I needed more.

"Ruby, do you want this?" Julian asked.

"Allistair..." I groaned, unable to reach for him or say more.

He raised his golden eyes to meet Julian's, asking his

permission. He must have agreed, judging by the rip of fabric as Allistair tore his shirt away. The sound of a zipper caused another wave of euphoria to wash over me and I pushed myself up, supporting my weight while Julian's rhythm never ceased. My lips hung slightly ajar and my eyes closed when I felt him before me.

I didn't wait for his instructions. I knew what he wanted.

Opening my mouth wider, I tasted the white drop of liquid on his tip as he pushed it in. A groan reverberated from him as I skated my tongue along the underside of his shaft, sucking him deeper. Julian was pushing me closer to the edge, literally and figuratively, my body shifting forward, slowly inching into Allistair with the pounding I was taking from behind.

"Are you going to roar for me, Ruby?" Allistair asked.

The hair lifted off the back of my neck as Allistair wrapped it around his hand, using his grip to pull my head back and widen my mouth. I wasn't prepared for the brutal assault of him slamming to the hilt in one go. I gagged once, trying to breathe through my nose, the orgasm creeping up on me slipping through my grasp because of it. I growled around him and his cock twitched at the back of my throat.

Bastard.

"I want to hear you roar for me like you did for him," Allistair's voice infiltrated my mind. He wasn't backing off.

I sucked hard and it drew a low hiss from his lips. He was close. Enough so that I could push it. I felt it as the pressure within him began to build.

The fingers on my clit stopped and I felt another sharp smack on my ass.

I groaned at the heat that quickly followed in its place. My body was becoming rapidly addicted to the little bouts of pain Julian liked to inflict. The way it shattered all rational thought, forcing me to succumb.

"He asked you a question, Ruby," Death commanded behind me. He pulled out entirely, his tip just sitting at my entrance, waiting for me to comply.

"*Fuck you,*" I snarled internally at Allistair for pushing, and Julian for pulling away.

The second blow that smacked my ass had me gagging and my abdominal muscles clenched. There was nothing hard or heavy inside me to tip me just over the edge into oblivion. I groaned in frustration, Allistair still in my mouth, his breaths becoming labored as a fine sheen of sweat trickled down his lower abs.

They were going to draw it out of me, one way or another.

Fire licked inside my veins, crackling to life around me.

"Put it away, Ruby," Julian demanded.

I swallowed hard as Allistair was pulled from my lips and the next smack reverberated through me. I could hear the air whoosh before another followed, hitting my upper thighs this time. So close to where I wanted to feel him. Heat blossomed in my skin as I tried to rein it in, to pull the fire back.

"I said, put it away Ruby. *Now.*"

His power slithered over me as he rained down blows on my ass. It hurt like hell, but I didn't want him to stop.

In a backwards way, it wasn't him that held the power in this. But me. In pushing him, I was also pulling. I encouraged the slaps. I relished in the stinging bite of his palm, knowing that some depraved part of my soul had guided us both here, and in the fire within, I found silence.

I tentatively reached out towards the flames as if they were an extension of myself, similar to the beast in that way. The banter and thoughts flowed between us quite easily, maybe the flames could too. Far too exhausted to fight his command, I pulled on my link with the flames and the beast, urging them to retreat.

No one was more surprised than me when it worked.

The beast wore the slightest of grins, something akin to pride coming from her.

I blinked through the tear-stained haze, only just realizing that the blows had stopped. My ass was going to be so fucking sore—

The bed shifted as Julian moved away, leaving me rather deprived of attention. That was not what I wanted out of this.

I groaned as I pushed myself up to a sitting position, sweat and tears plastered my hair to my face, and I raked a hand through my tangled locks. Out of the corner of my eye, Julian moved around the bed, coming from behind me to stand off to the side. His body was massive and gleaming in the pale moonlight coming from the windows. On his chest, over his right peck, a silver skull glowed. His brand, I realized.

Was he going to—

"No, I am not the one who gets to brand you first," he responded.

From the shadows, another fair-haired demon stepped out, but this one gleamed like gold. Shirtless, in nothing but a pair of well-worn jeans, Rysten walked up to the edge of the bed.

"Hello, love," he whispered softly. Leaning forward, he gently took my face between his hands and kissed me. I reached out, wrapping my arms around his shoulders. The kiss deepened as our tongues intertwined. The beast growled in approval.

Behind me, the bed sank. I pulled back slightly, trying to see who it was, but Rysten held me firm. Strong hands and an aura like honey touched mine as Allistair's hands roamed down my bare back.

Was he going to—

"No," Rysten answered my silent question.

His lips left mine to trail down my neck, two sharp points dragging against it. *His fangs,* I realized with a startle. I'd never seen his fangs.

Rysten stepped aside and Allistair pushed between my shoulder blades, guiding me down to my hands and knees. He rubbed his palm over the warm red skin on my ass and his fingers deftly spread my cheeks. I tried to clench them shut from shock, but it was already too late for that. Something wet and slippery slathered over my rim as Allistair's breath fanned the sensitive patch of skin just below my ear.

"Laran got to be branded first," Allistair said.

My breath hitched as something pressed against me, sliding in and stretching me; too small to be his cock, but too insistent to leave even a shred of doubt about how this was going to go.

"Julian got to fuck you first, and repeatedly," he continued, pushing and twisting two fingers in and out of me. The feeling turned from uncomfortable to downright pleasurable just as Allistair stopped his ministrations and pulled away.

"Rysten will get to brand you first, after you accept him."

The smooth tip of him pressed against me, and that scream from earlier...the one I hadn't been willing to let loose...it was starting to form again as he slowly pushed his way in. I made no move to stop him as a burning sensation filled me, and it wasn't fire. Rysten's dexterous fingers grounded me as they trailed across my hips and slowly skated between my already wet folds.

"I get to claim your mouth and your ass before the others, just to keep it fair."

My lungs were going to be bloody shreds by the time they finished with me. Fuck, I might have loved and hated them at the same time in that very moment. Allistair grunted as he settled inside me. I scolded myself to not pass out as he began slowly moving.

Too full. I breathed heavy. In. Out. In. Out.

There was too much sensation. I wanted it all, but it brought me to the teetering edge of madness with how they touched me, and broke me, and pieced me back together again. A scream ripped from my throat as Allistair thrust into me once. Twice.

"There is my roar," he groaned in satisfaction.

His cock stilled inside me again, giving me a chance to adjust. I leaned forward wanting to pull away, but not wanting it to end. Allistair made the choice for me, pulling halfway out before thrusting back in. The painful feeling mingled with a sliver of pleasure.

I had been on the brink of release, and all the pent-up frustration from Julian's hand had been torn from me, so I was left behind a trembling mass of limbs that shook with exhaustion, and I had no choice but to want and take what they were giving me.

Allistair scooped his arm under my torso, lifting me to my knees, my hands coming to rest on Rysten's chest. My watering eyes met his while he silently pried apart my swollen flesh, filling me with his fingers just as Allistair picked up his pace. He placed one hand on the curve of my neck as he kissed me. I moaned deeply, pleasure sinking its claws into my body further.

He tasted of wine and blood, a strangely erotic combination. His tongue slipped past my lips, entwining with mine as he drew me deeper into the cloudy haze where words would no longer suffice. On my knees before them both, I gave myself over, arching my back for Allistair while leaning into Rysten. One hand went up to rest on the curve of his chest where it dipped just below his throat.

The beast nodded in approval, guiding me as fire kindled beneath my palm. Rysten wrapped his hand around my throat, applying pressure and his fingers twisted around my clit as my orgasm rapidly tore through me, Allistair cursing as my muscles spasmed and tightened around him. He slammed his cock into my ass once more, finding his own release.

Kama filled the air, pressing into my skin. I relished in the feeling of Allistair behind me and Rysten in front of me as I branded fire and magic into his skin, claiming him as my mate.

The hand on my throat tightened as an unfamiliar energy washed over me. It filled my blood with darkness and shadow, infusing my very soul with a raw energy that grounded me. It was the calm after the storm. The midnight breeze that called. Whereas I filled him with fire and life, he filled me with peace and darkness.

And deep within, the beast and the flames settled as she sighed happily. Truly content for the first time in twenty-three years, in the arms of our mates.

ALLISTAIR

She was truly insatiable.

I'd never met a succubus that could push me to my limits. She put out enough kama to keep me fed just by standing in the same room as her. After a week, I had to claw my way out of her bed, leaving her with Rysten and Laran just so I could get a word with Julian.

"Any word on Bandit or Moira?" I asked him.

I had to keep my voice down, even on the porch outside with several walls between us. One never knew what abilities might come out during the transition, and the last thing we needed was her sent into a rage this deep into it. How the beast had managed to keep it together without us spoke to that entity's power and control.

"None," Julian answered.

I nodded once, because I knew what that meant. Someone had likely seen them with Ruby and trapped them.

"Has Sin found anything?" I already knew the answer, but I needed it off my conscience. I needed to know that we were trying every avenue to find her familiars.

"Not that she's reported. She said the trail ran cold at the underground. She suspects Le Dan Bia have them now, but being what she is, she's unwilling to enter to find out." Julian was able to detach himself from this because of the blood magic that linked them for the duration of her transition. He had difficulty focusing on much else. That was not the case for the other three of us. We knew what we would face when she found out.

Transition or not. Beast or not. She was not going to take that information well.

"Ruby might try to kill one of us when she finds out," I replied, and Julian nodded.

"I'd expect nothing less. Good thing I cannot die."

The same could not be said for her familiars.

CHAPTER 15

I FLOATED ON SMOKE. OR MAYBE I WAS FLYING.

It was hard to tell as I looked down at the world below. Blanketed by a moonlit sky, blue flames ravaged a forest. In that sky I sat, watching it all burn. Normal fire needed time to catch and grow into an all-consuming beast, but the flames of Hell were not normal. They did not operate that way. Instead, all that they touched instantly turned to ash as they swept across the land.

The beast felt a small thrill at the scene below, but I didn't share that with her this time. I did not wish that. Fire was life and light and cleansing, but it was also deadly and destructive. The winds blew warm air across my skin and layers of fabric drifted around my bare legs. Two long drapes of cloth hung over my shoulders and barely covered my breasts. It was cinched around my waist with a dainty gold belt. The onyx cloth wrapped around my calves, curving around my ankles. I was sitting on smoke, or a cloud more likely, given that the flames didn't give off smoke. Where I was or how I'd gotten up here was beyond me. I felt a steady unease that this wasn't right. Here, wherever I was, didn't deserve to burn.

I reached out to the flames below, calling them back to me. They stilled in their rampant destruction. A very clear line between all that had already burned and the world beyond that still could. I couldn't let that happen. The same as they were mine to unleash, they were also mine to control. To prevent from destroying everything.

I held onto that thought as I pulled them in, only then noticing the beast's smile.

"You are ready," she whispered.

I blinked, and when I opened my eyes it was the midnight sky that greeted me. Millions of little white lights lit up in constellations that you couldn't possibly see in any city. I stared at them for a moment in awe.

"Ruby!" someone shouted.

I blinked again and looked to my side. Dark glitter covered the ground as far as my eyes could see. It sparkled beneath the night sky, reflecting the stars above.

What in Satan's name had I done this time?

I yawned deeply and stretched languidly like a cat before pushing up off the ground into a sitting position. The Four Horsemen stood in front of me, each of their expressions ranging from bad to worse. I knew I was in deep, deep shit, and I hadn't even consciously done anything this time.

I groaned against the stiffness in my legs as I moved to stand. I'd fallen asleep and set everything on fire again, that much was clear. I was also stark naked, and I felt sticky between my thighs. That probably had to do with the ungodly amounts of sex I'd been having for...well, I don't know how long. I just couldn't seem to get enough. After Rysten branded me, it all got a little wonky. I remembered skin, lots of skin, and the distinct taste of each of their kama—and lots of biting, maybe some blood...aw hell. I was a filthy slut and they totally just went with it.

What's the point in being a demon queen if you couldn't act a little sinful sometimes? My new position was beginning to grow on me and it had a lot more to do with the four in front of me than any crown.

"How are you feeling, love?" Rysten asked, walking forward. Also naked. They were all naked. Hmm... I swallowed hard, averting my eyes from skipping from one male's package to another.

"I'm—" I coughed like I smoked a pack a day for twenty years. "My throat's dry."

Rysten nodded like he expected this and leaned down. Instead of just offering me his hand like a normal person, he scooped me up in his arms. I flailed, not all that much a fan of being picked up. I get that lots of girls loved that shit, but I was tall. That saying about tall people? The bigger you are the harder you fall? For someone who spent a lot of time falling, I had found that to be quite true.

Rysten locked an arm beneath my knees and wrapped the other around my naked back, cuddling me to his chest even though cuddling was the last thing I felt like.

"Put me down! You big oaf—" I elbowed him in the chest and Rysten sighed.

"You think you can manage not to burn anything else down for now?" he asked lightly.

My brows furrowed as I narrowed my eyes.

"Maybe..." I trailed off, opening my mouth to continue when the air whooshed around us. Instead of standing—or being carried like a lazy fuck—in the middle of a burned down clearing, we were now standing in a familiar living room. Rysten carried me to the couch as Julian stepped out of the shadows behind him. A ring of fire appeared to our left and Laran came striding through with Allistair. Rysten laid me on the couch almost gingerly before pulling away. He flipped the light on in the kitchen and started rummaging through the fridge.

This was weird. So weird on so many levels.

Allistair moved to pour himself a glass of scotch and settled in the armchair across from me, his half-hard dick was more distracting than I think he realized as his eyes raked over my naked body. We were gross—disgustingly gross—and yet, I probably could have ridden him right then and there without a care. I must have officially lost it.

Julian came out of the kitchen carrying a glass of water and two little red pills. He handed them to me silently and walked away as I downed the water and what was probably ibuprofen in about three seconds flat. To top off the strange atmosphere, Laran picked me up despite my grumbling and repositioned himself next to me with my head resting on his chest.

Hmm...maybe losing it wasn't so bad.

One of his arms snaked around my waist and the other pushed my mass of hair aside. His fingers trailed down my neck to the muscle where the neck and shoulder meet, slowly massaging out the tension. My toes curled inward as I let out a small moan of relief, and the very odd, fairly normal atmosphere froze as one of the other three turned to look at us, and Julian shot him a death glare if there ever was one.

What happened to sharing? I mentally sighed, not really giving a damn.

"He only likes sharing if he's involved," a warm voice echoed.

I jumped in surprise, looking around before I realized it was Laran. The whole mind speak thing was going to take some getting used to.

"Telepathy," he answered aloud, still addressing something I clearly hadn't said but trying to freak me out a little less. I relaxed back into him, and he continued with the massage.

"So, you can hear my thoughts now?" I asked. Around the room, each of them nodded and I twisted my lips. "Then why can't I hear all of yours?"

"You shouldn't be able to hear ours unless we send them to you, but you seem to be projecting yours while also listening into ours."

Allistair seemed troubled by this. A thin tendril of wariness wrapped around him. Hesitation.

"This bothers you," I commented.

The scent of fresh coffee came over me as a sizzling sound filled the air. My eyes swept to the kitchen where Julian was filling a giant coffee mug while Rysten fried something that smelled suspiciously like bacon. I wondered if it was Saturday...

"You displayed a lot of abilities during the transition. While it's not expected that you will keep them all, you showed many to such a degree that it is unheard of..." His voice trailed off as Julian filled my vision. He silently handed me the cup of coffee, holding out his other hand to take the empty glass. I traded with him, muttering my thanks as I took my first sip of pure heaven in far too long.

"Why wouldn't I keep all of them?" My mind seemed to snag on this. *Did that mean I would lose the fire? If I lost that—*

"You won't lose the fire, Ruby. Any abilities you displayed before your transition will still be there, just stronger now. Some things you were able to do during should have also stayed, others probably not."

I nodded along even though that didn't make a lick of sense to me. Why would I keep some and not others? That seemed dumb. Allistair sighed and Laran let out a chuckle. Apparently, they thought that was funny.

"During the transition, a demon takes on every ability in their genetic pool. As your body starts to change to fit immortality, the weaker ones don't usually stick. Instead, that energy gets absorbed in the process and repurposed for other things. Like accelerated healing."

While his explanation made sense, my body was clearly not doing its damn job. The ache between my thighs, while not painful per se, was not exactly pleasant. Allistair cut me a ruthless grin and Laran's hand tightened around my waist.

"You're not completely through the transition yet," Allistair said by way of answer.

"Yet?" I asked. He nodded, and I took another swig of coffee.

"You went through the worst of it at the cabin. At this point, you shouldn't have more than a day left before you'll be feeling better than ever. Until then your body will need a lot of sleep and food—" His eyes flicked down to where I was licking my lips. Just the mention of—"Real food, not just kama," he inserted tightly.

The tension in the air thickened, his cock hardening to a thick column. Kama pulsed from behind me, as Laran's magic hands pulled the tension from my shoulders. It brushed over my skin, turning my brain to mush for a second.

In the kitchen, a bang and loud cursing pulled me out of it. I looked up to see Julian giving Laran another death glare, followed by a mental threat he probably thought I didn't hear. I grinned to myself, hiding it behind the lip of my coffee mug as I took a long sip. The bitter burn did just what I needed it to, clearing my head of more thoughts of sex.

"So..." I drawled out. "Why did you take me to the cabin and not back here?"

"We didn't have a structure strong enough to hold you," Julian answered from the kitchen. He came out holding a plate of bacon and lifted my feet to sit at the end of the couch. "We had hoped this one would be with the wards, but after you broke out the first time, I wasn't chancing it again."

Broke out? Ha! I whooped their asses and jumped

three stories like a boss. Nice way to downplay it, Julian. Real nice.

Allistair choked on his scotch and coughed twice as Rysten grumbled in the kitchen. It was only Laran that sounded half as amused as I was when he let out a deep laugh.

"So you took me out in the middle of the woods, so I couldn't run? Or if I did, it's not like I had anywhere to go…"

Julian nodded, offering the plate of bacon. I happily took it and began munching away.

"You know that's creepy right? You literally took me to the middle of nowhere, so you could—"

"Fuck you?" Julian said, staring at me without remorse.

I shrugged. Fuck me. Smack me around. It wasn't all that different when I was doing it with him. The dark glimmer in his eyes told me he heard that and had plans for a lot more fucking and spanking. I shivered, and it was entirely out of desire. Not an ounce of fear.

"We also had to get you away from the city, love. There were too many people that would have died if you decided to go all supernova in your sleep," Rysten added, walking into the living room while scratching the back of his head.

On his chest, just below the dip in his throat, a dark blue pentagram swirled like smoke. On one hand, it looked kind of cool because brands never did that. On the other hand, my fire didn't have smoke, so I don't know why they kept manifesting that way. He took one look at the seating arrangement and moved to sit on the adjacent couch.

I knew that demons felt quite comfortable in the nude, but this group nudity thing was taking it to a new level. I would need some time to get used to this new dynamic.

"We have all the time in the world now, little succubus, once we—" Allistair cut off short, his eyes flipping to Julian. I frowned, tilting my head sideways.

Were they really trying to keep things from me again? What the shit—

"It's not what you think," Laran said. His hand drifted over the tops of my shoulders as he tried to massage the tension out. His chin sat just on top of my head, where he'd tucked me into him.

"That would be easier to believe if you four didn't continue to keep secrets and try to control every aspect of my life," I replied, more than a little salty.

Mates, we may be. Perfect, they were not. Or sane. Can't forget that one.

"We only do it to keep you safe, love—"

"Cut the shit, Rysten," I snapped. Something was missing here. Something so obvious, it was right in front of me... "Where's Moira?"

Silence.

Looks like I was getting to the crux of it on my own.

"Where. Is. Moira?" I repeated. She was my familiar, devil-damnit. If they won't tell me, I could find out myself. Opening my mind, I reached out, trying to feel—

"She's going to find out anyways."

"And heads are going to roll when she does."

"The banshee made her choice—"

"—Moira is her familiar, as is Bandit."

Laran was the only one that didn't think of my raccoon as vermin. Speaking of—

"Where are Moira and Bandit? Where are my familiars..." My voice trailed off as a scene appeared before my eyes.

Back in the underground, Julian had grabbed me. I remembered him grabbing me, I didn't realize Bandit had fallen off when he did. He scurried out from between our feet and dove into the mob. Where no one had seen him since...

...or Moira.

I blinked, my body lurching as I pulled away from Julian and the memory cut short. He was really going to regret binding me with blood magic, because the transition wasn't over, but they were missing—and now I knew it.

MOIRA

I picked through the remainder of the half-eaten turkey sandwich one of the guards had been eating last night. As unappetizing as it was, it was still food, potentially the only food I might see for forty-eight hours. Not that many people brought things down here from the world above, outside of strippers, booze, and bait for their barbaric ring.

I'd been trapped in a ring much like this as a child, time and time again. Now, no one knew I was here. I was free to walk and to wander and to watch, but they couldn't see or hear me, and I couldn't directly interact with them—me and the trash panda.

In the asshole's defense, his skills at finding trash to eat for both of us had been coming in handy down here, not that I ever expected to need it. I was just happy the little bugger seemed concerned enough with keeping us both alive that he thought to share instead of keeping his rump fat and happy. Although, he did make a better pillow when he was.

I tore the sandwich in half and handed one to him. Bandit wrapped his paws around it and started scarfing it down. At least my opposable thumbs were useful in taking water bottles from the bar and keeping us hydrated. Not that it stopped the guards from emptying out the water bowls I made for him because they thought they were trash. I was over this fucking curse two weeks ago. Lifting my wing, I glared at the rune on my back.

Fucking Fae. Fucking Seelie.

I swear, when I get out of here—and I will—someone was going to die.

"Take it from someone who knows, the Fae are not the easiest to kill."

My neck actually cracked from spinning around so fast and Bandit leapt to my defense.

"You can see me?" I was in complete disbelief. After two weeks of being nothing but a ghost, this had to be a hallucination. Only my imagination would come up with a woman that beautiful that could speak to me in my darkest hour.

"I can, but I'm actually here for him." She pointed a purple claw towards the trash panda and something about it jogged my memory.

"I've seen you before," I said to her. She smiled a little vixen-like and snapped her fingers. The clothes changed from dark fighting leathers to a pair of tight jeans and a cropped shirt that read 'Voodoo Doughnut' in Pepto-Bismol pink. "*You!*"

"Me," she agreed, nodding her head like this was amusing.

"What are you doing here? And how can you see me?" I asked, narrowing my eyes. After talking, and screaming enough, I'd finally figured out how to control the sound waves to some degree, but it was easier to ignore them entirely given I couldn't do a damn thing about my curse.

"The whys and hows aren't all that important." She swiped a clawed hand out and caught Bandit faster than he could react. The raccoon twisted to bite her, but she was already pulling away. "I'd perk up, though, if I were you. Ruby will be here soon."

She disappeared like she'd never been there to begin with, but even in the dark light I didn't miss what she'd taken from Bandit. Hairs. Five little blue and black hairs.

I pulled the raccoon to my chest, feeling protective over him. Because whatever she came for, she got it, and I had a bad feeling about what might bring Ruby running.

CHAPTER 16

"You left them at the underground!" I screeched. It wasn't a question.

I jumped away from the couch, landing on my still wobbly feet. The plate of bacon tipped off the couch, falling to the floor where no one reached for it. All eyes were on me as I crossed my arms over my chest and glared daggers at Julian. Sure, they were all at fault, but it was Julian that had them call off the search.

Laran. Laran had been the last to come to me in my transition. He had stayed out the longest to search for Moira and Bandit, but it appeared they were gone. Except I knew that couldn't be true because they were my familiars, and if they were in pain at any point, I would have felt it...wouldn't I?

Shit. Shit. Ball-licking bastards—

"I can assure you I don't lick balls," Allistair inserted.

I rounded on him with my cup of coffee still in hand and did the only thing I could think of.

I threw it at him.

I threw my perfectly good, hot coffee at his face and stood my ground. I didn't even have the fucks to give to run like I probably should have.

"You bastards left them there!" I yelled.

Something flickered deep inside me; not the beast, and not the bonds with the Horsemen. Something else. Someone else.

I pushed it aside, almost positive it wasn't Bandit.

"We didn't want to leave them, Ruby, but you needed your other mates—" Julian tried to interject.

"We seemed to be getting along just fine without them," I snapped. Okay, maybe not the greatest insult ever, but I was so beyond angry. *Moira and Bandit were out there somewhere, probably scared and lonely and—*

"I highly doubt the raccoon is scared or lonely, love. He's a wild animal. He can survive outdoors." Rysten's words did nothing to calm me. I knew he didn't like Bandit, but I didn't give a shit. "And the banshee is a legion now. She can take care of herself—"

"You left my *familiars* in an underground fighting ring that takes pleasure in *killing*. Do you even understand the gravity of this situation?" I asked, true hysteria creeping into my voice.

"We didn't abandon them," Laran started. I turned to him, my hands clenched at my sides, not amused in the slightest if this was some kind of joke. Whatever he had to say, it better be good. "We called in a friend of ours to find them. If anyone can do it, she can."

She? Something ugly touched my chest. *Jealousy.*

Allistair chuckled under his breath, despite the coffee dripping down his body.

"What the hell is so funny to you?" I snapped at him.

"You. I can't believe you're feeling jealous after the two weeks we've just had," he continued laughing under his breath, but my insides furled at the horror in his statement.

"They've been trapped in the underground for *two weeks?*" My voice didn't rise this time. There was no hysteria. Only the bone chilling cold of what I'd done.

Moira, who had been so scared she could barely move when we went down there...she was trapped. I just knew it. Why else would they not be able to find them?

"We don't know they're down there." I heard the words but tasted the lie beneath them.

"Where else would they be?" I replied coldly, all but calling him on it.

"They could have escaped, love—" Rysten stopped talking when my dark gaze flicked to him.

"You don't believe that any more than I do."

"I'm sure they're fine—" Allistair started to say and I finally snapped.

"Don't tell me that!" My head spun as power gathered inside me. Fire licked at my skin, burning away all the unmentionable substances coating it. "Stop telling me what to think or how to feel because you guys fucked up. *Again.* You knew better than to leave them down there. I would rather transition and be in pain than have you abandon them down there. You fucking knew," my head swung around savagely to stare at Julian. He did know, but he also cared so little for most things outside of me, his brothers, and his duty, that it wasn't at the forefront of his mind during our time together. He had such an easy time making the call, he didn't even regret it.

"You left my best friend and Bandit in an unfamiliar city. The Gates of Hell, no less. You left them in one of the nastiest fighting rings on the continent, where either one or both could be..."

My throat closed up. I couldn't afford to think like that. I couldn't afford to let anger or jealousy or anything else cloud what I needed to do.

The atmosphere in the room quieted.

I stormed off down the hallway and into the first bedroom I saw.

My mind was racing through a million scenarios as I ripped open the drawers before me. I dressed without thinking or feeling...no, that was a lie. I couldn't not feel, but what I did...it hurt. The Horsemen had done a lot of crazy and stupid things. I had too, but this decision stung like betrayal.

It's not like they didn't know she was there, or Bandit. They knew, and they still chose to leave. No matter the reasoning, that was unacceptable. Moira wasn't just my familiar, she and Bandit were my goddamn family and if they couldn't learn what the hell that meant, then I wasn't going to waste my breath.

"Where are you going?"

I couldn't see them, but I knew which one asked. Only one of them would phrase it in such a way as to make me question myself. They knew what I was going to do, and somehow, he made it sound like a threat.

"I'm leaving, *Death*," I spat. "Someone has to go find Moira and Bandit."

Part of me felt like I was being a bit harsh. I mean, the beast was the one that brought them, and I was the one who wanted to go down there and deal with Le Dan Bia to begin with, but that didn't excuse the blatant disregard for their lives. It didn't excuse that Moira may be down there being tortured, or worse...

Someone rested a hand on my shoulder, but I shrugged them off, pulling a tank top over my head. On top of the dresser, a stack of hair ties sat. I stole two and pulled back my ratty hair. It could really do with a good wash, but that would have to wait. Moira was out there somewhere, and Bandit too.

"Ruby." Another hand grasped at my shoulder and I tried to shove them off. Once again, whatever strength I had before was gone. Maybe that was one of the powers I wouldn't get to keep. That kind of sucked if it was the case, but it's not like I got to pick and choose. That's life for you.

Rysten stepped directly in front of me as I moved to the doorway. I knew it was him by the pentagram on his chest and the white brand on his arm. It looked like some sort of biohazard symbol with rings encircling it. I stopped before running smack into his chest, but I didn't look at him. I didn't want to. Rysten was sweet and kind and...manipulative. He knew what it meant to be human. He knew how to play with my emotions better than any of them. Twenty minutes and enough self-doubt and they'd be trying to lock me away again, convincing me they could sort out this mess. I wasn't having it. Not now and not ever.

"Ruby, love, I'm not trying to manipulate you," he whispered. He lifted one hand to the side of my face in a sweet gesture, his thumb brushing over my cheek. I stupidly leaned into him before I could stop myself. Slapping his hand away, I shook him off and took a step back.

"Don't 'love' me, Pestilence. She's my best friend, and Bandit's...well, *pet* doesn't quite cover it, but he's important. They're family, and I'm not leaving them out there while I finish the transition."

Rysten sighed deeply and someone stepped up beside him. I lifted my chin just enough to see his honey-colored eyes.

"If you try to put me to sleep, I'm castrating you, Famine," I growled. A little bit of the beast crept through despite the blood binding. With my transition coming to an end, the spell must be weakening.

"I'm not going to put you to sleep—" He broke off abruptly and both he and Rysten turned around as one.

What were they doing?

Julian was gone first with the others hot on his heels. I stood there dumbfounded.

Was this all a joke to them? Did they think it was funny?

I followed after, prepared to give them a piece of my mind if—

I stopped dead in my tracks because standing in the living room was none other than the girl from Voodoo Doughnut. I say girl, but her eyes held a lifetime or sorrow with the hardness to withstand it. She wore dark fighting leathers splattered in blue. Demon blood. My thoughts went silent when I saw what she was carrying in her arms.

My heart stuttered once. Then twice.

It was a lump of fur, both blue and black. His head lolled to the side, and though his limbs were shaking, they were losing energy fast.

Water pricked at my eyes as I ran to him. Because I knew. I knew deep, deep down what this meant.

I stopped a few feet away and the Horsemen remained silent. Failure ripped at their hearts. It wrapped around them, squeezing so tight it—

I pulled away from them. I didn't want to hear it. To see it.

"Give him to me," I demanded. My voice shook with pain and loss and a sorrow that very soon would consume me. The silver-eyed woman walked forward and placed him in my arms.

A prickle of life flared inside him as she handed him over, but it wasn't enough. It wouldn't be. With him in my arms, I could see the deep gashes and red blood that his fur had hidden.

The woman spoke, but I didn't hear it.

I registered that the Horsemen were talking. Saying something.

But I didn't hear it.

Someone had hurt him.

Someone had killed him.

I looked at my familiar. My raccoon. My Bandit.

And my heart broke as the last sliver of life left his eyes.

I could heal a soul, but I couldn't save a body.

I could burn the earth, but I couldn't save him.

And in that moment, I knew that a part of me was going to be forever changed.

I readjusted him in my arms, unable to see much of anything past him through the blurry tears in my eyes. Placing one hand on his chest, I pushed forward whatever energy I could. Wishing his soul healing and peace as the light faded from him.

It was blue, the same color as my own.

And when it died...

Something inside my chest unfurled, dark and ugly.

Someone was going to pay for this.

Someone was going to die.

"Who did this?" The voice that came out of my mouth didn't sound human, but it wasn't the beast. This was fury that she would let me act on alone.

The woman stepped forward, her face unreadable. Impassive.

"I found him in the underground hosted by Le Dan Bia. They put him in the pit with a hellhound and..." The woman looked to the Horsemen behind me, not wanting to say what I had already put together. "Moira asked me to bring him back to you before he left this world."

Though grief and despair had me, my mind pulled apart the pieces of information I needed. I was correct that they had never escaped Le Dan Bia. How the Horsemen had never found them...I wasn't sure what to think of that. Only that there was more at stake than setting a precedent. They had killed him, and Moira hadn't come back.

Why?

"Why isn't she with you?" I asked.

Question. Information. The pounding in my chest told me I only had a small grasp on the fire itching to leap out at them.

The Horsemen had left him. I had left him.

The pounding quickened.

"She was trapped in a cage, but alive. I could not bring him back and save her. She asked me to bring him so that you could say goodbye." I grimaced. Moira had chosen to stay in her own nightmare, so I could see Bandit one last time.

A small light filled me at the selflessness of that act.

I would save her, and I would kill every single one of them doing it.

"Ruby, you need to think about this—" Julian placed a hand on my shoulder that I stepped away from, a cold resolve settling over me.

"We may be bonded, but you are *not* my keeper," I snapped. A tendril of something far from sanity was wrapping its way around me. Around my words. I didn't try to push away that sliver of darkness. That sliver of shadow and night that Rysten had branded onto my very soul.

"It's not safe," Julian insisted. He tried to take a step forward, but one dark look from me was all it took to stop him in his tracks.

"You do not get to decide what is safe or not anymore. You have failed." There was a hardness inside of me that would not break under him. Under any of them. "I am the heir. I am Lucifer's daughter. Not you." He flinched under my words like I'd struck him. In truth, that would have been kinder. "They took him from me. They killed him, and I am not going to stand by and just let that go. I'm not going to let them take Moira too."

There was something scratching and clawing and screaming inside of me now.

Vengeance.

"Le Dan Bia are going to learn what it means to cross the Queen of Hell, and you can stand with me as my mate or you can continue to sulk, but I've made my choice."

With that, I turned to the strange woman with silver eyes and white hair. The purple ends were flecked with blood. Blue and Red.

She stepped up holding out a hand. A silent gesture that she would take me where I wished to go. As far as the Horsemen were concerned, I had no idea who she was. Clearly, they knew more of her than they'd clued me into. So, I guess I wasn't the only one keeping secrets.

"Wait," Julian said. I paused and only half turned to him.

His jaw twitched with anger. I knew with great certainty he was itching to argue and then fuck me six ways to Hell. Now wasn't the moment, and he knew that.

He felt it. My grief. My rage. My despair.

He felt it all because of that damned blood bond he'd forced on me.

And it was coming back to bite him.

"Yes?" I asked, my voice as cold as the bite of death that clung to us. Him and I.

"We're coming with you." That's all he said. No apology. No groveling. No brave words or promises he couldn't keep.

He was coming with. Him and my other mates. I looked from one to the other, waiting for looks of affirmation from each of them.

Maybe they knew I didn't want words. That there was nothing any of them could say to make this better. Only actions. I wanted to see that they would stand by me. That they would fight with me. That in the end, they would not attempt to stop me.

Because even if they tried, they couldn't.

Not right now. Not when my emotions were so far gone, and a whisper of insanity was beginning to wrap around my pain-filled soul.

No. Right now there was only one thing that would make it better.

That was the blood of my enemies.

They moved quickly, dressing themselves much as I had. Dark jeans. Strong boots. My flimsy tank top wasn't ideal for what was to come, but I was very much aware of the fire pulsing beneath my skin. These clothes likely wouldn't last long.

Neither would Le Dan Bia.

And very soon, the legions of Hell would know that their Queen was not simply a girl that ran, but a living, breathing woman who wasn't afraid to burn the rot of evil out from whatever cesspool it came from.

I was done running. I was done hiding.

I was done holding back.

CHAPTER 17

I STOOD IN FRONT OF THE DARKENED ALLEY. LAST time we were here I thought the beast crazy. Sure, I had wanted to free the Fae, something I fully planned on doing once Le Dan Bia were taken care of—but I hadn't had the guts to really stomach what went down below the streets of New Orleans. Monsters in the night. The things that made even demons afraid.

Yes, I hadn't been prepared before.

This time I was.

Julian held his hand out for mine, and Death and I walked into the shadows like two old friends. The heat of my transition didn't burn within me as sorrow weighed on my soul. Only ashes and darkness.

Desolation and destruction.

Rage...and desperation.

A scream split the air the moment we stepped back into existence.

A scream that hit me square in the chest. My heart

thudded and a sheen of sweat broke across my skin as I took her in. Demons of every kind swarmed. They poured from the walls and the shadows. They sent spikes of poison and souls of the dead. They mounted at every point of the room, to attack.

And Moira, she wasn't locked up like some caged animal.

She stood at the center of it all. Wings of fire snapped from her back and the brand on her forehead glowed. A determined glint lit her brilliant blue eyes as she assessed the demons coming for her. There had to be hundreds, and the only thing keeping her alive was that there were so many—too many for them to effectively attempt to dispatch her.

Well, that and her scream.

They ran for her and from her, but none could touch her. Anything that came within ten feet found itself exploding in the weight of her sonic scream. The demons began crushing each other as the makings of a stampede began. Moira launched herself into the air, soaring straight to the ceiling.

How she had survived even a moment down here was beyond me, but I would make sure it wasn't for nothing.

Above us, a portal of fire licked at the ceiling. The flames burned a deep orange and red. The demons below shouted obscenities, but nothing they said could prevent Laran and Allistair from falling through.

They landed with a boom and the real fighting took off. That was our signal. Our time to move.

I willed the fire to life as an extension of myself and my hands lit up. The demon nearest us didn't have time to react until he was burning, and by then it was already too late. He dropped to the floor in agony that would continue until the flames ate every bit of him from inside out.

Did he play a part in Bandit's death?

I didn't know. I didn't care.

Acting without remorse, I flung the fire wide around me. It inched its way up my arms a little higher, a little hotter, as bodies exploded in clouds of black glitter.

One after another they met a horrible end by my hand, so fast that the air didn't even smell like burnt flesh. Only sweat and blood and agony. Because they'd put me in a blind rage that I could not and would not contain.

Someone grabbed me from behind and I sent an elbow back into their throat. The weight trying to pull me disappeared instantly as I turned and flung another wave of power.

In my dreams I had done this and more quite easily. I destroyed an entire cabin and parts of a forest without realizing it. But that kind of fire didn't come from this kind of raw pain. Every one of them was another slice to my chest that I could not seem to heal. Someone here had killed Bandit. Maybe more, but I'd never know who. I'd never be able to pick them out and make their pain last longer. Make them fear their death whilst they looked me in the eyes.

For all I knew, the person responsible died by War's wrath, a single swing of an axe and they would be beheaded for good. Or maybe it would be Rysten, who infected them from the inside out, festering deadly diseases that ate their bodies faster than any poison could.

Allistair's methods better suited my tastes for revenge, the way he walked without lifting a finger and bodies dropped. He sucked the emotions from them like a leech. Stronger than any incubus, he left them with nothing. No sense of self. No cognizance of life. They simply fell to the ground with eyes wide open. It should have disturbed me, but it wasn't so different from what one does when their soul dies. They felt a pain and loss so deep that they often couldn't even scream, and then there was nothing. My fire eating at them was probably a relief and I hated that. I hated that no matter what I did, it didn't make it better.

Killing them didn't make it better. Letting them live wouldn't make it better.

Nothing could fix this broken hole inside of me where Bandit should have been.

With that thought, the fire inside died out. I turned with my heart only half in it, and maybe that's why I wasn't surprised by what came next. I wasn't shocked by the ripple of pain that spread through me, not so great that it could overrun the emotional state I was in, but strong enough to eat through the adrenaline.

From above, a banshee screamed, and I looked up, expecting the pain to not be mine, but hers. The thought filled me with true terror, until I saw that she was fine and well. She glided to a stop, her flaming wings flicking embers into the mob below. She was dressed in the same clothes she'd been in the night Julian took me. Blood flecked at her feet and shins, but her skin was unmarred. She was untouched.

So, what had caused her to scream in such anguish?

My eyes fluttered as I worked to draw my gaze up to her face.

Now I saw the absolute horror that had made her scream.

...it was me.

I stumbled forward, following her line of site—straight to the spike sticking out of my stomach.

I swallowed hard.

Not good. This was not good.

I had taken out demon upon demon this night, but a spike slipped through. One that undoubtedly belonged to a chupacabra. Their venom was poison to demons. Not enough to kill the immortal, but enough to seriously injure.

And me? Was I immortal yet?

I didn't know.

My head spun with the horrible truth, but I could not bring myself to simply stand here and wait to die. Despite the exhaustion creeping in, I willed the fire forward. More. Faster.

It burst forth from my chest in a wave of unprecedented power, spreading outward. It crawled up the walls and onto the floors as I used everything I had to incinerate the entire damn building.

One way or another, I was ending this. My knees shook disjointedly as I took another step forward. It seemed that my body no longer wanted to support me. In fact, I no longer seemed in control of it at all.

The world tilted on an axis. My vision faltered. My legs failed.

I only briefly registered the crack that rang in the air.

Was that my head? My darkening vision led me to believe so.

Was this it? Was tearing apart Le Dan Bia all I accomplished as Hell's Heir?

Somehow that seemed like a crock of shit.

What was the point of being some precious heir if you couldn't ever do anything?

I swore to myself then and there, that if I lived, I was embracing this destiny. That if I survived...I would wipe out the evil in both worlds on my path to the throne.

And as the darkness closed, I prayed that if this was the end, I would find Bandit on the other side. That we would go wherever comes next together. And that the Horsemen—however misguided they were—found peace and happiness. That they didn't blame themselves. That Julian wouldn't succumb to guilt. That Rysten would hold onto his humanity. That Laran would trust again. That Allistair wouldn't try to drink himself into oblivion.

That Moira didn't blame herself.

The darkness wrapped around me, and that tendril of shadow and night held me close.

But even deep in the recesses of my mind, I heard it.

I heard a monster roar.

JULIAN

I'd lived what the human world would call a thousand lifetimes. I'd seen wars fought. Kings rise. Devils and empires fall. I'd endured more than my share of hardships. I've died a thousand deaths or more.

Never once in my life had I felt an all-consuming fear.

Until now.

A gnarled spike, two inches in diameter, protruded from her stomach. And even through the bodies of demons moving to run away from her, I could see every glorious inch as she lit up. The beast couldn't come out, but she didn't need to anymore. Now that Ruby knew how to control flames, even dying, she was going to make it count.

It started with a glow beneath her skin. Her eyes turned an iridescent blue, reflecting an unnatural light. There was determination and pain painted on her face. She clenched her fists together, and the shift in the

229

atmosphere was sudden. Flames shot out from her, but unlike the fires that she started while sleeping, these flames took the form of animals—raccoons—as they chased after every demon attempting to flee. They traveled so swift and sudden that the concrete began to crack as the structural integrity became compromised. Her power blasted down the floors and up the walls and through the ceiling. It covered every inch of visible space so that in that moment, all I saw was her.

Then she fell.

I couldn't say what happened around her after that. I couldn't tell you if the roar that followed was me or one of her other mates, or even her familiar. I just ran, skidding to my knees in time to catch her before she cracked her head on the craggy concrete.

She blinked. Her eyes already glassy as she stared up at me unseeing.

"No-no-no-no-damn it, Ruby—you can't do this—" It wasn't even a choice in that moment for me to even consider grieving. She couldn't leave me. She couldn't leave *us*.

I couldn't allow that.

The spike in her stomach said otherwise as blood started to pour out, oozing to fester around the wound. Beneath the smeared blood, her skin began to turn black. Poison.

I swallowed hard because there was only one way she would survive this.

There was a reason I didn't brand her first. In fact, I intended to be last. To be branded by Death was more than by any of the other Horsemen. It was something I wanted to talk to her about. To let her have the choice, since I took her choice in everything else.

It was meant to be a gift, but now that was taken as well.

She had to live. That was where I drew the line.

Which meant she had to change.

I pulled the stake out and tossed it aside, placing the palm of my hand over the wound that now gushed blood and poison. I siphoned off a piece of my own soul with my magic and pushed it into her.

Branding with a mate was a special kind of process because you gave a part of yourself, and in doing so, you made a part of them like you. I was more than a necromancer, but there wasn't a word for what I could do. The way I could exist, both dead and alive. In the veil, but not.

No other necromancer could defy Death, but I was the exception. I earned my name. I made my name.

Her skin felt cool beneath my hand, but the black poison was starting to recede. While the wound still gushed blood and gore, the magic of my soul was now planted within her. A piece of me for the piece of fire she gave me.

That is what separated mates from other types of bonds. There was a give and take that did not come easily or naturally to demons. Even many harems in Hell consisted of one demon taking pieces from all of their partners, but never giving. With mating, it was a choice.

And I chose to make her immortal.

Truly immortal.

CHAPTER 18

A LOT OF PEOPLE TENDED TO SAY SOMETHING profound when they were dying, these calming strung together thoughts that really made no fucking sense to me. Things like 'Death was easy. Life was hard.' When really that couldn't be further from the truth. Death was the end. It was permanence. Beyond the veil where I wavered was an endless existence of drifting. Would I retain my mind? I had no fucking clue, but I didn't trust it. Not one bit.

Here in this place of existing and not, there was no pain. At least not physically. I walked, but there was no floor. There were no people. No voices. No whispers. Not even that all too famous bright light everyone liked to claim they saw.

There was nothing.

Nothing but me and endless darkness.

I lifted my right hand and called forth my fire.

Against the murky black depths, it was bright. So bright that I winced before extinguishing it. As much as it sucked, the darkness was better. The beast agreed somberly, shifting inside me.

That seemed strange to me. That here I was, wherever this was, with a body I was certain wasn't actually real—that the beast would still exist within me. If this was some corporeal dream, surely she could have her own body? Or would she even be here at all?

Again, I wasn't sure, but I didn't trust it.

Something just seemed wrong.

Do dead people normally have this much presence of mind?

"You're not dead."

My head snapped up and I turned, looking in the direction the voice had come from.

Standing in the darkness, a glowing white figure dressed in blood and leather walked forward.

Voodoo Doughnut girl.

My would-be assassin-turned-savior.

"Where are we?" I asked, my voice echoing off of non-existent walls. This was weird...

The mercury-eyed woman crossed her arms over her chest and flicked her long, sleek ponytail over her shoulder. The ends were white, not purple as they had been only hours ago. Which meant—

"We're not real, you and I."

She smiled, not quite cold, but calculating nonetheless. In her eyes were secrets that many had died for, ancient truths I could only hope to learn. This woman was old and powerful. She was unlike any demon I'd ever known.

"Very good, Daughter of Hell. We aren't real. Not in the sense you are thinking, anyway. This place is the in-between. The veil."

Ice slithered through my veins. So I was that close to death—but what was she doing here? Wouldn't it be more fitting to find Julian? She cocked her head, examining me with a peculiar interest.

"It would be more fitting to find Death here—were you going to die. As it is, he's currently occupied with removing the spike from your stomach. Nasty poison, that is, but you'll be fine."

Okay, now this was really beginning to freak me out. The Horsemen had said I was picking up on their thoughts. That I was projecting my own. But if I didn't have a body, and we were in the veil—shouldn't I have been able to shield myself or something? Was that even a thing?

The woman continued to stare at me. Somehow calling her that didn't seem like enough. She was certainly not a girl, but nor was I sure she was a demon. Blood magic wasn't a gift that demon-kind held. Which made me think that, like me, she was something *other*.

Something...different.

"Who are you?" I asked. She considered me for a moment.

"My name is Sin, but that's not the question you want to ask." She spoke with more than confidence. It was an eerie wisdom. The distinct sense of knowing that the person before me was not all she seemed.

"*What* are you?" I corrected. She nodded; that was the question she expected.

"That's a secret. One you are not ready to know."

I frowned, blowing out a steady breath. Okay, back to the riddles, I guess. Her vagueness didn't bother me as much as it should have. She was supposed to be an assassin, after all, one that not so long ago was sent to kill me. Yet...neither the beast nor I sensed danger from her. While she was dangerous, that knife point wasn't currently aimed our way. That didn't mean I trusted her, but an ally didn't necessarily need trust to be worth listening to.

"I was stabbed. I'm pretty sure that's why I'm here. What it doesn't explain is why you are too. Which makes me think it has something to do with me. Why are you here?"

She inclined her head and rocked back and forth twice on her feet before coming forward. Closer.

"It's hard to explain, given that I don't understand it completely myself. Last time I saw you, we entered a blood oath, with you owing me a favor. I sealed the oath, closing a tiny sliver of my magic inside you. That sliver was supposed to stay there. Dormant. Waiting until I called upon you, where it would ultimately be released back to me."

"Okay," I drawled. "But I nearly died and you're the one I'm seeing. I'm not sure how a tiny sliver of magic does that."

"You entered the transition less than twenty-four hours later"—she paused when I opened my mouth to ask how she knew that, but then closed it as soon as I thought

about who I was dealing with. Of course she knew.
—"And proceeded to make your presence known all
across New Orleans."

She shot me a less than amused look and I, unlike the
beast—whose fault it was— at least had the good graces to
blush and look away. It had not been the smartest of
choices.

"I'm still not seeing the correlation here—"

"Sometime between when I left you and when the
Horsemen called me in to find you, you started using
magic you shouldn't hold. Magic that is very dangerous
for you to possess, should my master find out." She raised
both her eyebrows, prompting me to follow her train of
thought. Willing me to come to...

I came up blank.

Sin sighed, uncrossing her arms to roll her shoulders
back.

"You somehow took that tiny scrap of magic inside of
you and synthesized it."

Oh...was she saying that I copied her magic? How
was that even possible?

"Um...you do realize that I'm a demon, right?
Demons can't use—"

"*Most* demons can't use blood magic. A select four
that we both know of can. They were created that way so
that they could bind you. As they tried. However, you
were able to break it—not because of your sheer strength
—but because you possessed an inkling of my magic and
multiplied it. The blood oath is still in place. You did not
absorb it or break it. You simply...copied it, as you say."

She frowned, and I got the feeling this woman did not show her emotions easily. Something about this troubled her.

"You said that it's dangerous for me to have it..." I started, a little unsure with how to phrase this.

"If my master learns what you possess, we are both dead. There is not a world where your guardians will be able to hide you that *she* will not find you," Sin replied swiftly, without sparing me anything. I grimaced at the implications. Clearly, I wasn't dead now but that could always change at the drop of a hat. Things tended to do that in my life.

"Then I hide it. That shouldn't be hard to—"

"You will not be able to hide it. The Horsemen already suspect, given how strong your telepathy is. The thing you call mind speak, where you are able to listen in, is something that I exclusively can do. Which only leaves one option..."

I took a step back, raising my hands in front of me. I seriously did not like the sound of that. Anytime someone used ultimatums, it tended to end with something about killing or torturing me. I didn't care who she was, or how real or not this body may be. If I wasn't dead yet, I was going to attempt to stay that way.

"Listen, you may have helped me out a few times, but I..." My voice trailed off when she lifted her hand and began to draw.

Was she—no.

No. That was not possible.

I know I said and thought that before, but this—her—

I couldn't even finish that thought before the shapes she drew became indigo-colored symbols in the air. A moment later, I felt a pop in the space around me.

I shook my head, not liking the sudden onslaught of dizziness.

"What did you do..." I muttered, pressing my palm flat to my temple and rubbing it in circles.

"Silence. I ensured that neither your thoughts nor your bonds with the Horsemen would give you away. After you wake, they will no longer be able to hear your thoughts, nor will you hear theirs. Should you try to speak about it, you will find yourself unable to. It will be like this meeting never happened."

I backed away, trying to shake my head, but found myself getting more and more dizzy. How was that even possible? How was any of this possible?

"They cannot know, Ruby. No one can. You are the future of Hell, and I am not willing to sacrifice that or the future you will buy me by allowing you to get either of us killed."

My world spun in circles as the heavy fog in my brain dragged me down...down...under. It wrapped around me like a blanket, lulling me to sleep.

But I didn't want to go. I couldn't. Not without knowing one thing first.

"Are you a..." The final word never left my lips. It seemed the ability to talk was now one I also did not possess.

Sin stared at me with heavy resignation and a tinge of sadness in her eyes.

"Goodbye, Ruby. Until we meet again."

And with that, my eyes fell shut and my consciousness faded.

CHAPTER 19

WHAT WAS THAT GOD-AWFUL SCREAMING?

I tried to roll on my side and burrow my head under my arms, but a sharp pain in my stomach, like something tearing, snapped me right awake. I blinked twice, using one hand to wipe at my eyes. The sheer amount of ash and grit was an assault to my senses, making my eyes itch and water. My throat was dry as the desert sands. What was it they said about Hell? Endless torture where you will beg God for just a single drop of water? While the sentiment held true, that wasn't what was going on here.

For one, I was pretty sure Hell didn't have ten-foot tall raccoon breathing fire...

My eyes flew wide open, trying to take in every detail of the scene above me. Standing next to me was a black and blue striped raccoon so large I could ride on him. His face was set in a fierce expression as he zeroed in on something just beyond my vision.

I groaned, having a bad feeling upon seeing pretty

much the entirety of the room had exploded into ash. Few things were immune to the flames of Hell.

"Now listen here, vermin," I heard Rysten's voice carry. I could imagine his hands held up in surrender as he inched forward. "Ruby isn't doing well right now, and I need to get to her—"

"Bandit?" I murmured. The raccoon sat back on its haunches and turned to look at me. Unnaturally blue eyes with pentagrams in them stared back at me. His ears twitched in recognition and he lowered himself to the ground, nosing me gently.

I nearly sobbed in relief as I tried to pull myself up into a sitting position, but a strong hand on my shoulder held me down. I groaned from the strain and turned my head sideways, only then realizing I wasn't flat on the ground to begin with. My head was resting in Moira's lap while Julian kneeled at my side. Behind him, Laran and Allistair stood watching me with worried expressions. I didn't want to read into any of their faces or emotions. They were all too heavy for the elation that was growing in my chest.

Bandit was alive. He was—

Currently jumping to snap at Rysten again for trying to get too close.

"What in Satan's name did I do to deserve this treatment while the overgrown trash eater runs wild..." Rysten muttered.

I chuckled under my breath and my throat itched, causing me to descend into a fit of coughs that triggered a terrible pain to rip through my stomach. I moaned, cringing into Moira's lap while she brushed my hair back from my face.

"Hey, Rubes," she said softly. "I thought we'd lost you there..." Her voice trailed off instead of saying things that were better left for later when it was just the two of us, not that there was any guarantee I was getting alone time anytime soon.

"I imagine I'm a bit harder to kill now," I rasped, smiling wide despite the pain in my stomach. Moira grimaced while looking down at me, lifting a single delicate eyebrow. She knew exactly what I was feeling, whether I faked it or not. Blasted familiar bond.

"Not hard enough. I don't know what you were thinking coming here," she said. I frowned. What I was thinking?

"You were trapped. Of course I came for you."

The Horsemen stilled beside me. I inched forward, opening my mind to them...only to run into an invisible barrier.

Damnit!

Sin wasn't joking. I don't know what she did, but whatever spell she cast over me definitely wasn't letting me listen in. Just when I was getting used to it too. Ugh. She and I were going to have a chat next time we met, about what she did to me and why.

I got the distinct feeling she was leaving a lot of information out, but until I better understood my abilities and *how* I originally copied her magic, I wasn't getting any answers. Not like I could mention any of this to anyone, since she so conveniently made sure of that.

I needed to find out more about Hell and who might

possibly be after me. Sin was powerful enough to get around the Horsemen entirely, and even she feared her master. That didn't bode well for me, and as much as I begrudged her for doing it without asking, if people knowing really would put an even bigger target on my back, I was probably better off with her blasted spell. Not that it would stop me from cursing her to Eve and back when we met again, because we would. I had no doubts about that.

"How did you know that?" Moira asked sharply, breaking my concentration.

"Do you remember that demon from Voodoo Doughnut?"

Her eyes darkened, and her mouth tightened. "She came to you?"

I nodded, and Moira turned away, hiding the troubled expression in her eyes. I reached out, opening my mouth to ask her what was up right as I heard footsteps. Suddenly, Bandit wasn't the only one growling. I turned, catching only a brief glimpse between my overgrown raccoon's legs.

"Eugene?" I asked. The air around us thickened, and while I couldn't hear their thoughts, I could sure as Hell feel their emotions.

Jealousy and possessiveness took over, and I knew without a doubt they would kill him. If not them, then Bandit or the growling banshee beside me.

Shit.

"Ruby?" Eugene called. He didn't take the time to explain why he was here or what he was doing. That was his first mistake. His second was not thinking before walking toward the snarling raccoon. Bandit reared back, a growl ripping from his throat. Next thing I knew, blue fire was shooting out, and despite the damn hole in my stomach, I'm sprang to my feet.

"Stop!" I shouted.

Everyone froze.

I took that split second of silence and inaction to inhale a deep breath, deeper than it appeared my body wanted to take. I bent at the waist wheezing, and a wiry arm wrapped around my midsection. She grasped my arm and tossed it over her massive wings, draping it around her shoulder. I gave her a painful grimace as thanks and hauled myself up to a semi-decent position. The Horsemen closed ranks around us, with the exception of Rysten who was now beside Bandit, as a united front against the very large—but not so smart—rubrum.

"What are you doing here, Eugene?" I called out in a rasp.

He blinked sheepishly and ducked his head, still awfully oblivious of the raccoon creeping forward to bite his head off. I reached out and placed a hand on his furry black and blue tail, patting him reassuringly. Bandit stopped his advance and sat back on his haunches. Again, my throat thickened as my eyes pricked with unshed tears.

He was alive. I didn't know how. I saw him die. I saw his soul die.

But he was alive, and I could only assume magic had something to do with it given his new size and the fire.

I turned my attention back to Eugene who was looking increasingly uncomfortable at this point.

"What is that *male* doing here, Ruby?" Julian asked like it was *my* fault.

"Can we kill him?" Laran asked in complete seriousness.

"What?" I stumbled forward to try to put myself between the idiot demon and my mates, temporarily forgetting that pesky hole in my stomach and a ripping pain tore through me. "Motherfucker—no you can't kill him! Bandit—don't you dare!"

Bandit stopped his creeping and gave me an annoyed grumble, except it was a hundred times louder now that he wasn't the size of a large cat. I rolled my eyes. Only my raccoon would almost die and come back freakishly large with fire and still have an attitude problem.

"Eugene, if you can't tell, this isn't the best time. Why are you here?" I asked, putting a hand to the shrinking hole in my stomach. It was closing. Slowly. That meant my transition was nearing the end, even if dark blue blood was still dripping down my fingers from where I was applying pressure to it. Getting stabbed with a poisonous spike was high on my list of things never to do again.

"Donnach sent me," Eugene said. His lips pressed into a sad almost kind of smile. "He wanted to remind you about your deal." The rubrum shifted uneasily, and it hit me that he wasn't as clueless as he seemed.

"I see..." I said slowly. "Well, it doesn't look like any demons survived, at least up here. I assume he must know that already if he's willing to send you all this way."

Eugene gave me a pained look and I got the impression that despite what I'd done for him, he didn't want to be here anymore than I wanted him to be. Donnach must've really wanted those Seelie freed.

"It shouldn't be too hard freeing them now..." I trailed off at the swell of emotions coming from not only Bandit and Moira, but the Horsemen as well.

"Your deal? What is he talking about?" Rysten asked without looking away from Eugene.

"The beast and I sort of made a deal with this guy named Donnach to free the...people they're holding here. That's why I was here the night you guys came for me."

No one called me out on my hesitation, but the smooth hands running along my bare hip bones wasn't just for the hell of it. Aged scotch, heated seduction, and something wholly sinful settled over me.

"Why can't this Donnach free them himself?" Allistair asked, his voice singing with the smallest hint of persuasion. I leaned into him, pulled by the power that lured me. He brushed my hair aside, letting out a low chuckle in my ear. Moira bristled beside me and Julian let out a grumble, snapping me from his spell.

Unfortunately, Eugene was not so lucky to escape Famine's charm.

"Donnach couldn't free them without risking a war with demon-kind," he answered, scowling deeply in confusion. I turned and whacked Allistair on the arm, but I may as well have hit concrete. The slap echoed in the dark and muggy underground.

"Why would there be a war?" Laran asked, a hint of a growl in his voice.

A sigh escaped my lips. I really should have known I couldn't keep it from them.

"Because Donnach is Seelie and the Le Dan Bia captured a number of his people to use in their fights. They're being held here underneath the pit and I have to free them." I paused at the indignant sighs and grunts from the Horsemen. No one outright told me I couldn't, but they weren't thrilled with this new development. "He swore under magic that his people wouldn't hurt me once I freed them, and as the future Queen of Hell, I felt like it was important not to start my time by blindly turning an eye to shit that demons aren't supposed to be doing to begin with. Maybe my father did, but I'm not that kind of demon, and I refuse to be that kind of Queen."

From in front of me Rysten's shoulders slumped a little. "I suppose that means the rubrum has to remain intact?" he asked under his breath, but I didn't miss the thinly veiled threat. Rysten, the sweetest of them, was not pleased about Eugene's presence. Even more strange, I couldn't tell if their possessive nature was grating my nerves or if I was beginning to kind of like it...nope. Definitely couldn't be that one. Grating, it must be.

"Yes, I would appreciate you guys not being assholes. The beast and I are not interested in mating him for devil's sake." I rolled my eyes and Eugene froze, his eyes going wide.

"You guys thought—" He broke off looking back and forth between me and the Horsemen, then to Bandit who had gone back to growling at the red demon. "No, no...I owe Ruby a debt. She saved my soul. I swear on the sixth ring where I was born that I have no interest in laying a claim on her...I'm also gay." He looked downward, no longer wanting to hold eye-contact now that he realized what all the puffed-up chests were about.

Not my almost dying, but his maleness.

Assholes.

"If we're all done asserting who is and isn't Ruby's mate, can we get on with freeing the damn Seelie so I can get some sleep. I'm fucking exhausted and I need a steak," Moira grumbled. I can't say I faulted her. All I wanted right now was a cup of tea, a hot bath, and a warm bed. In that order preferably.

"This way," Moira said, taking the lead. She led us to the door behind where the bar used to be. Now only piles of ash and concrete remained. As a group, we walked over to the dark hole in the wall.

"You've been through here." It was less a question than it was a sad statement.

"I wasn't in a cage," Moira assured me, and I frowned. "I'll explain it...later." Her eyes shifted towards Eugene. She didn't trust him. Rightfully so.

We followed her down the stairway to a deeper part of the underground. My breath came in short pants from the physical exertion it took to get down there. Because hobbling on flat ground was apparently too much to ask for.

"You okay, love?"

"I'll manage," I replied through clenched teeth, trying not to let the pain bleed through into my voice or my actions. Moira slowed her step, waiting for me to catch up at the bottom, and wrapped an arm around my waist to help brace my movements. "Thanks."

"Don't mention it," she muttered.

Laran touched my arm. I knew it was him by the warmth of his hand and scent of wildfire.

"Allow me." He moved by us, taking the lead. I didn't have the strength to keep them from 'accidentally' harming Eugene, free the Fae, and argue about coddling me. I'd been stabbed and had come close to death. So this time I suppose it wasn't really coddling. Not when I put it that way.

A ball of flame erupted in the air and he suspended it on his way down, lighting our way to the bottom. We followed after him with the rest of the Horsemen behind us.

At the bottom of the stairs, a rusty metal door blocked our path. Or it did until Laran kicked it down. The door itself didn't open, but the stone wall it was set in cracked at the force of his blow. The surrounding rock split and the entire frame as well as part of the wall came crashing down. A plume of dust kicked up and I hacked and coughed until it cleared, Moira holding me up through it all.

Fire shot out from his hands, massive glowing orbs of red and orange hovered several feet off the ground, illuminating the metal bars and causing screams of panic around us.

I gasped, but Moira didn't make a sound.

She knew what was coming. What awaited us in the dark.

Cages. So many cages. They lined the walls, stacked on top of each other from the floor to the ceiling. Most of them were empty. Most, but not all.

As Donnach had promised, four cages in the far

corner on the right held grey figures. Their black hair was scraggly and matted, their slate skin covered by only filthy rags. Black bruises adorned them, covered in healing cuts and fading scars.

It was horrifying. Repulsive. I had to fight the urge to vomit just thinking about the mess Moira came to me in, and as it was, Moira was staring down at them with a grim expression and bleakness in her eyes. Her arm around my waist squeezed tightly, as if she were holding me together. My steps trembled as we walked farther into the room, because in the back, something growled—low and deep—and with a purpose.

"We need to get them out and get out of here before that thing gets loose," Julian said.

No kidding. I squinted to see the far corner of the room, but metal bars and shadows masked it. Only the deep steady breathing of the monster gave any clue as to what was down here with us.

I stepped forward, examining the Fae in the first cage. She was a woman, not much older than me by the looks of it, but it was hard to tell when she was covered in so much grime.

I went to undo the lock on her cage, but there was only one problem with that.

It didn't have one.

No locks...and yet, the Seelie were very clearly trapped inside.

I stumbled forward with Moira at my side to better look at them. Laran followed, keeping close beside us. He reached forward trying to wrench the door open, but the metal didn't yield. It didn't bend. It didn't break.

That couldn't be good.

"Did the Seelie you made a deal with mention how you're supposed to get them out?" Allistair asked, coming up on my other side.

Two cages over, I saw Eugene attempt to phase, reaching through to rescue them. The floor dropped out from under him, but the metal bars stayed firm and didn't allow him access to the other side. He let out a grunt, holding onto the cage while lifting his legs out of the hole his power had created.

"No, he failed to disclose that information," I muttered.

Never mind the fact that if neither strength nor phasing would work, what chance did I really have? I could try to melt them with fire. It was unlikely to work and would probably injure or kill the creatures inside. I was pretty sure the cages were not only iron to weaken the Seelie, but they were somehow magically enhanced to prevent normal means of getting to them. Like phasing through shit was normal, but hey, for a demon it was.

"Do you know how?" I asked Moira.

She took a deep breath, her eyes as turbulent and troubled as a firestorm. "I'm not sure..."

That meant she had her suspicions. Moira stuck out her boot toeing the edge of one cage. "Hey, you," she said to the nearly catatonic girl. I would have thought she was dead if her pinky hadn't twitched. "Yeah, you. How do we open these cages?"

Another twitch. Her head slowly creaked to the side, and through cracked lips and a bruised face she responded.

"Blood magic," she spat the words with a venom I wouldn't believe possible since she was only moments from death's doorstep.

Moira sighed and pulled me away. Judging by the look on her face, she had suspected as much. Blood magic to open those cages could mean any number of things, and I didn't understand how to undo spells done by the Unseelie. Most demons didn't. The Unseelie were few and far between, almost as rare as the Seelie in that way. They kept their magic to themselves and so information about it was sold at a premium.

However, I'd met a woman who could do both kinds of magic. It made me wonder all the more.

We slowly backed away as her eyes fell shut again. The exhaustion was finally catching up with me. Between my dizziness and Moira's strange behavior, we moved further away.

"What are we going to do?" I asked, trying to block out the growling coming from the back corner. It was really creeping under my skin. "We can't just leave them here."

"Sure we can," Moira mumbled. I cast her a sidelong glare and she pursed her lips, sighing deeply. "I'm not saying we should, or even that I want to leave them here. This place is a graveyard. Souls linger here. The dead speak." She shook her head. "But blood magic is rare. The Unseelie don't just hand that shit out to anyone. I dunno. Something doesn't feel right here." Moira scratched the back of her neck, breathing slow. Watching everything. She was naturally more paranoid than most people, but I agreed with her. Le Dan Bia had been the largest clan on the North American continent for over a decade. They rose up from nothing and became the portal keepers, quickly amassing power. Now throw blood magic into the mix and...it was certainly enough to make one concerned.

I pressed my lips together and glanced over at Julian. I could ruminate on Le Dan Bia at another time. "Can you open the cages?"

Julian's jaw tensed as he took me in and he ran his thumb along the curve of his bottom lip. I shivered despite the sheen of sweat on my skin and heavy air, thick with swamp water and mosquitos. I sincerely hoped that Hell wasn't just a more extreme version of Australia.

I don't think I could handle the heat *and* everything trying to eat me.

"She said blood magic is what keeps them in?" he asked. I nodded once, and Moira's wing swept around the back of my body. "I can open the cages, but I want a promise from you first."

Of course he did, because what demon ever did anything for free? Just me. Ruby Morningstar, tattoo artist, Queen of Hell, and apparently, demon slayer if you have a good enough sob story. I could add that to the list of things I needed to work on.

"What kind of promise?" I asked him, stepping out of Moira's warm embrace. I had to pull my dirty locks of hair away from my face so that I could look up at him. Even with my tall stature, Julian was a giant.

"No more leaving us. No abandoning us for strange males," he said and cut his eyes sideways at Eugene. I held back the eyeroll. "No making deals without talking to us first." I leaned forward, both from dizziness and the uncontrollable pull I felt to him. "Yes, you're going to be Queen, and we will all need to learn how we're going to make this dynamic work..." His words trailed off as he took in the other Horsemen. I knew then he wasn't just talking about Moira or Bandit, but the four mates the beast and I had chosen. He drew his gaze back to me, a darkness smoldering the green in those dark depths. "But not for a second will that stop me from tying you up to my bed for three days."

I gasped... I couldn't tell if what I was feeling came from his words or the dark look in his eyes as he said them.

"Well, that's quite the list of requests."

"I'm not asking."

I swallowed hard and nodded. Yeah, we were getting there, but there was still a long way to go with him. With all of them, really...and we may never get there. But at least the sex would be great on the way.

"No, because that would be too normal for you," I sighed.

"If you want *normal*, you have Rysten," Julian replied. He reached out and brushed the back of his knuckles along my jaw before turning away without a word.

I swayed where I stood, watching Laran hand him his axe. Julian gripped the pommel with ease and then brought his hand down on it. A spray of fresh blood scattered over the row of cages. The metal glowed bright where the blood touched it. Julian handed the axe back and leaned over to wrench one of the cage doors open.

The girl inside lifted her head and looked up into the eyes of Death.

There was nothing fearful about her expression, nor was there any gratitude. Only a deep-seated hatred and loathing. He stepped aside to open the next cage and her eyes slid to me. Curiosity swept over her face as she assessed my presence. I inched forward around Laran, tilting my head to the side.

That's when I felt it.

Recognition.

"You're the Heir," she said. Her words were hardly more than a whisper, holding just the briefest hint of that strange lilt that the other demon hunters also had.

"Am I still the Heir if the King is dead?"

I don't know why I asked her that. Possibly because everyone referred to me that way, despite the fact that Lucifer was long gone. He'd died months ago now.

"Donnach was right about you. That you would be different." It was both an answer and not.

"How do you know I spoke with him?" I asked her.

She crawled out of the cage, rising to her feet. Shredded garments hung from her limbs, leaving her orange runes on display.

"Because I was sent here as a trial for you, and a punishment for me. I'm happy to see he was right, given that I would have been left here to rot had he been wrong." Her words sent me reeling and the gentle swaying of the room intensified.

When the moving stopped, and my vision cleared, I saw that the four Fae had been released and were grouped together. The woman raised her head again to look me in the eye. Never mind, the demon who had actually released her, or the giant raccoon I knew was prowling at my back.

"He wanted to test me. Why?"

She smiled, and it wasn't pretty. Her black teeth glinted in the low firelight, pointed and deadly.

"Because my brother wishes to return home."

She didn't give me more than that as she lifted her hand and began drawing. As with Donnach, the air thickened and the markings swirled together. A distinctive pop sounded, and magic exploded outwards. A small portal forming with only a light haze of orange between this dimension and the next.

"I don't even know what that means," I said. Each of the Seelie went before her until only she remained. She paused only inches from it.

"For now, it doesn't matter." The dark Fae woman lifted her hand and drew another rune. It floated before her, suspended in the air. "But when the time comes, I owe you a debt. Stay safe, Little Morningstar."

The flow of magic shot through the air, hitting me square on the shoulder. I gasped in pain, slapping my hand over it. It burned hot, hotter than the flames of Hell, that's for certain. I peeled my fingers away, flinching at the feel of the harsh air against it.

The skin was orange and glowing. A series of hash marks and interconnected lines that came together to form a rune.

Devil-damnit, how in Satan's name did this keep happening to me?

First the damned blood oath, and now this. I turned

to demand she remove it, but the girl was already gone—
and with Julian diving towards her disappearing figure,
the portal snapped shut behind her.

"What the hell did she do to me?"

Allistair stepped in front of me and pushed my hand
aside. His eyes crinkled in worry, but I knew it was more
than that. Inside of him, a deep concern was starting to
form the longer he looked at the rune.

"There's good news and bad news," he said eventually. I blanched and made an impatient grunt for him to
get on with it. A smirk tugged at his lips, but his heart
wasn't in it. "The bad news is I don't know what rune
this is."

Well, that was just flippin' great.

"And the good news?" I asked him, my shoulders
shaking with exhaustion.

"I know someone that can help us find out."

I nodded, reaching up to run my hand down my face,
rubbing the grit from my eyes. They stung like a bitch
after all of this.

"Well, I guess we can add that to the list of 'shit Ruby
needs to figure out'," I muttered to myself. He slid a hand
under my jaw, his fingers curling around my chin as he
tugged it upwards.

"We'll figure it out together, alright?"

He didn't leave any room for brokering when he
looked at me like that. I leaned in, unable to help myself
and let my lips brush across his. Allistair let out a small
groan, pulling my closer. One hand snaked around my
waist while he switched his grip on my chin to grabbing
the hair at the base of my neck.

My tongue slipped out, parting the seam of his lips—

"Ruby, babe, I love you to death, and you deserve some after almost dying today, but can this please wait until we are back at the apartment?" Moira interrupted.

I groaned, pulling away reluctantly. The world slid out from under me and I had to roughly grab at Allistair's shoulders as he supported me to stay upright. It seemed that both my head and my legs had decided they were done for the day.

The hands holding me changed from warm and butter smooth to delightfully chilly as Allistair passed me off to someone.

"She's still losing blood," Allistair said. I didn't like the worry I heard in his voice.

"Don't coddle me. I'll be okay..."

Still, even with my insistence, Julian hoisted me up, his arms gripping me under my knees and back. He cradled me to his chest carefully, a stern frown forming at his lips as he looked at the hole in my stomach. It was only the size of a dime now, but blue blood, black dirt, and all sorts of other substances were coating me. What I really needed was a damn shower with a fire hose.

"You're in pain," he said.

"I wasn't aware being stabbed was supposed to be pleasant," I responded dryly. Julian's frown deepened. Against my better judgement, I rested my head against his chest, fighting the wave of dizziness upon me.

"We're going to take care of everything, Ruby," Allistair said. His voice was low and sweet, but thick with a raw untamable power. I only realized what he was planning to do.

"If you put me to sleep, I swear to the devil I'm never sucking your cock again," I growled, snuggling closer to Julian. Like he would protect me.

"Darling, I don't have to do anything. You'll be asleep before we're even back at the apartment."

He wasn't wrong. Julian turned for my raccoon and the Horsemen began talking. Something about Bandit and not fitting in the apartment. Before I knew it, the darkness was fading in. Black swept up on me, but this time, there was a comfort in it. A solace. Instead of a desolation that crept through and left me isolated, it was a shadow that wrapped around me and comforted. A shadow that held a tendril of Rysten with his embrace, and a hint of something that hadn't been there before. Another kind of darkness that was strong enough to pull me into its depths and never let me go. A permanence of a sort. Almost like...death.

CHAPTER 20

FUR TICKLED MY NOSE. BANDIT. DEMON RACCOON couldn't just let me sleep—

I bolted upright in bed, remembering a second too late that I had been stabbed. I cringed, waiting for the pain to follow, but after a moment of sitting there, it never did. I looked down, expecting to see my own naked flesh, but a crisp white t-shirt hung from my shoulders. The material was long and baggy, it must have been one of the guys'. I tilted my head forward to smell it. Crisp. Clean. Just a hint of—

"Are you smelling my shirt?"

I froze, looking over to my left where Julian was leaning back against the black ebony headboard. His hair was smooth and blonde, not a hint of dirt in sight. He wore a snug white t-shirt, much like the one I had on, and dark jeans. His feet were bare, and as crazy as it sounded, he actually had attractive feet. Was that even a thing?

The bed we were sitting on had an ivory comforter. The walls were white. Startlingly so.

We were sitting like nothing had happened, clean as could be. I was confused as hell, but the first thing out of my mouth was, "Yup. Sue me."

Julian cracked one of those rare grins and shook his head. "I have better things in mind," he said huskily. My inner succubus purred and leaned toward him, but Bandit was having none of it. A disgruntled grumble sounded from behind my head and the air whistled past my hair as something just barely skimmed my scalp, and Bandit, now back to his normal size, was sitting on my lap.

"Bandit," I breathed happily. He looked up at me with those unnatural eyes. Blue with pentagrams, but past the blue and black fur, he was still my Bandit. Wiggling eyebrows and all. "He's small again," I said, having trouble asking the right question. My raccoon clawed at my shirt as he pushed himself closer and reached up to wrap his paws around my neck. I scooped him up in my arms, holding him there.

"Apparently the raccoon can now change his size, along with breathing fire," Allistair said. I looked up to see him standing in the doorway. "You must have imbued him with your magic, you or the beast."

"Mhmm," I drawled. "And coming back to life—did my magic do that to him too?" Bandit cuddled closer, letting out a purr.

"We're not sure," Julian answered. "I think it has something to do with him being your familiar." I scratched behind his ear while I thought about that.

"Does that mean Moira can't die either?"

If it did, that was one less thing to worry about in Hell. She was a banshee with the powers of the legion now, but she wasn't unkillable. Unless somehow the bond with me was what saved Bandit and could save her too.

"We're not sure," Julian repeated again. Firmer this time.

I rolled my eyes and filed that away under things we never test. Maybe it was. Maybe it wasn't. Somehow, I still came out of the transition with my soul and my familiars intact. That had to count for something.

"So..." I trailed off. "What happens now?"

Wasn't that the question of the day. What happens? Where do we go next? I suppose with both Moira and I having gone through the transition, the logical step was likely Hell. But what would we do there? And what about Sin and this mysterious master she keeps warning me about?

The question and uncertainty of it all made my head hurt.

Allistair cleared his throat in the doorway. "That's something we need to discuss, but first—hungry?"

He wore low-slung jeans that fit his hips well. This was the first time I'd seen him in anything so informal, without a shirt, no less. Not that I was complaining. He crossed his tan arms over his chest and the muscles swelled doing funny things to my libido. I licked my lips involuntarily when he tilted his head sideways and the curtain of dark hair moved with him. He arched an eyebrow in question.

Shit. He hadn't meant hungry as in sex. He meant food. Like, real food.

Of course, after a little group debauchery, my mind went totally to the gutter. Well, mine and the beast's. While I turned my face away to hide the scarlet that was no doubt creeping across my cheeks, *she* didn't give a damn at the forwardness of our assumption. In fact, she was more than a little eager for that, but we had things to discuss.

After that...well, I'm not a saint.

"I'll take some coffee, if that's alright." He nodded and turned to leave, giving me a nice view of his backside. Julian let out a small growl and I glared at him. Arrogant, possessive shit.

"Last I checked, you all agreed to this arrangement, and you really didn't seem to mind sharing back at the cabin," I grumbled.

Bandit started wheezing again as he let go of my neck and rolled backwards onto my lap. Damn raccoon. He *was* laughing. Was that a thing? Could raccoons laugh?

I guess he could, just like he could breathe fire and change size.

"I chose to be bound to you of my own free will, just as you have chosen the four of us as mates. Does that mean you will always do what we ask? Clearly not, or you wouldn't have almost died on me." I swallowed hard. How was it that he could take an offhand comment and make it something so deep and raw? "Just as that doesn't mean that we won't have our issues with possessiveness. Demons don't naturally share, Ruby. The most powerful of us form harems, yes, but most are for strength. Not...this."

Ahh, and we have now come to the heart of it.

"But you want this," I said.

He nodded. "I do. Just as Rysten, Laran, and Allistair do. We are males in our own right, and while they may be my brothers in guarding you, sharing your bed won't always be easy." He paused, running a hand across his jaw. "But most things in life aren't."

I took a deep breath and let it out, feeling my shoulders relax a little.

"We'll find a way to make it work," I said, sounding surer than I probably should be about this. "Make it... fair." I liked the sound of that. Apparently, Julian did too because he grunted in acceptance and moved to stand.

"That's all I ask. I'll leave you two to talk." With that, he walked out of the room, nearly plowing over Moira in the process as she came into my line of site. She side-stepped around him, drawing in her massive wings. It was an awkward motion, but leagues better than I would have expected from a girl who only had them a few weeks.

Being trapped in the underground may have forced her to learn. The thought settled over me like a grey cloud, leeching away the ease I had been feeling.

"How're you doing?" she asked. She wore a white tank top and her dark green hair was pulled into a messy top knot, two dark blue horns sticking out in front of it.

"Shouldn't I be asking you that?" I answered softly. She pressed her lips together and looked away. "I'm sorry, I—"

"Don't," Moira replied swiftly. She sighed and placed a small hand over my arm. "Please don't apologize. You didn't know that would happen. It's not your fault."

"We were down there because of me—"

"Ruby," she insisted. Her tone was stern but edged with weariness. "The demons didn't trap me. I wasn't kept in a cage. I was..." she paused, swallowing hard. "I thought I died at first. I could walk and talk and touch — but no one knew I was there. No one but Bandit and one of the Hellhounds they kept caged. I ate their food. Smashed their liquor. I even slapped one of them, but no one could interact with me. They thought I was a ghost." There were shadows in her eyes as she looked at everything but me. Her posture was too stiff as she rocked back and forward on her feet. Being down there may not have killed her, but there were walls around her mind now. Walls around her heart. Walls where there shouldn't have been, not with me.

"I don't know what to say," I told her truthfully. I had no idea what I was supposed to say if she wouldn't let me say I was sorry. "I feel like it's my fault for why you were down there, and while the Horsemen carted me off, you were stuck—"

"I wasn't stuck," Moira said. She turned to the side and lifted one flaming wing. I blinked once and swallowed.

"That's a rune."

"I think Donnach used his Fae mojo so that I couldn't leave. Bandit has one like it on the bottom of his back-left paw." She turned again, tucking her wing around herself.

Was it a subconscious act? Did she realize how her mannerisms had changed already?

I didn't know, but I sure as shit wasn't comfortable with the red-colored rune on her upper back. I didn't speak the language of the Fae, either race, but the mark that looked like a bird cage wasn't hard to understand.

"So, he spelled you to keep you and Bandit there. How? I was watching him the entire time—"

"I've thought a lot about that, and the only time I think he could have was when we were transported, before we came to our senses. If Bandit had been paralyzed as well, then we might not have noticed..."

Her logic wasn't bad, but if it were true...who knows what else he could have done. Where else there could be marks on our skin. I ran a hand over my shoulder, feeling violated even though it wasn't me he marked.

"It was premeditated. He planned to make sure I would enter the underground and save the Seelie one way or another. I don't see how he could know that, though," I sighed. A knock at the door drew my attention. Allistair extended a pale hand holding a steaming cup of black coffee. I took it and smiled gratefully.

"Everything alright in here?" he asked, far too casually. Moira picked a piece of lint off of her leggings, turning aloof. I nodded to him and he turned to leave. "I'll let you two catch up then..." He trailed off as he awkwardly left.

"What are you thinking?" I asked her, moving to take a seat on the giant white bed. Moira picked at her nails while she weighed her thoughts back and forth. Paranoia and distrust was eating at her.

"It's going to sound crazy," she said. I smiled at that.

"I'm sure I've done crazier." A slight grin tugged at her lips, but only for a second.

"I think Eugene was a plant. That the Seelie man somehow orchestrated this entire thing. You trusting the rubrum. Him transporting us to him. Appealing to your humanity to get you to go into Le Dan Bia and release his people..."

She was right. That did sound crazy, but that didn't mean it was wrong.

"I don't know how he could have done it. I know that by forcing us to stay there, it was his guarantee you would be forced to come back and deal with them. There's something missing..." She took a deep breath, gnawing on her lip thoughtfully. I trailed my hand over Bandit's fur and he rolled onto his back so I could rub his tummy. That red rune she told me about flashed into sight and my hand stilled. A thought clicking that hadn't been there before.

"You said Bandit was also with you right? That he couldn't get out?"

"Yeah," she nodded. "They couldn't see or interact with him anymore than me. When he thought you died, he lost his shit and grew, that was the first time they seemed to notice. They saw me when you crossed over the threshold, so I can only assume that's when the spell broke on both of us." She glared over her shoulder at the rune on her back, her arms tightening around herself.

"It's—"

I choked. Blinking rapidly, I doubled over and coughed hoarsely. Moira walked around the bed and took the cup of coffee out of my hand before I spilled it. She clapped me on the back, waiting until the hacking subsided.

"You alright?"

"Yeah, I was trying to tell you it's—"

I choked again. The coughing came harder as I struggled to breathe. My chest tightened, and a dread settled in me. I knew what happened. Or at least pieces of it. Enough that *she* knew I would figure it out. That I would piece together what happened with Donnach and her own uncanny timing as she delivered what I thought to be Bandit's body, moments after we returned from the cabin. We'd just been arguing about me going to find them when she showed up. Julian wasn't going to let me go. The others probably wouldn't have either, and then I thought Bandit died and I lost my fucking mind. But if Bandit was trapped there the entire time, she couldn't have brought me his body, which meant she somehow brought me something that looked and felt like him in every way—and made me think he had died. That Moira was following.

I don't know how, or why, but she did.

Tears blotted at the corners of my eyes and I stopped trying to fight it. The invisible silence that she'd forced upon me. I wondered if the rune was somewhere on my body. I'd have to look for it later.

"It's what?" Moira asked me after I'd been sitting in silence. There was no way to tell her the truth, but I didn't have to feed her lies.

"It's a mindfuck," I said. She nodded her head agreeing and handed my coffee over, falling back some into the conspiracies her own mind was spinning. It made my head hurt to think about it. To wonder how far back it started. To deduce where happenstance ended, and Sin's planning began—her and Donnach. I wasn't completely sure, but I had an inkling of what she might be, and if I was right—if she was helping Donnach—I took a long drag of coffee and swallowed hard.

"If Donnach did spell you," I paused as her eyes darkened, "why do you think he did it?"

Moira blinked, trying to follow my change of questioning. Or at least that's what I thought she was confused about as she squinted a little and furrowed her eyebrows.

"He wanted the Seelie released, obviously."

"Yes, but that's short term," I said, thinking out loud. "The Seelie girl made it sound like it was more. When I asked her why she said, *to go back home*. What do you think she meant by it?" Again, I had a suspicion, but I didn't want to be rash in my assumptions.

"Everyone knows the Seelie came from Hell, but what's that got to do with you saving his sister's sorry ass from the bait ring? It doesn't make sense, but I get the impression they don't want it too either."

I nodded. We were agreed then. It was Hell she was talking about. Where else could it be? They came from Hell. That was their world, and Lucifer and Lilith booted them out.

It's not really surprising that they would want back in, but I didn't see what we'd have to do with it and how me releasing the Seelie played into it. Or really, me having Julian release them since he gave the blood.

We fell into a nice sort of silence. The kind where I gave Bandit belly rubs and he purred so loud it filled the void that might have been awkward otherwise. Moira let out a tired breath and sank back onto the bed beside me.

"Do you want to talk about it?" I asked. She stared at her hands as she twisted them round and round.

"Not particularly. You feel guilty and I'm not in a place to comfort you and deal with my own stuff." She unclasped her hands as if she'd just realized she'd been fidgeting. "It's a shit situation no matter how we look at it."

"Yeah, it is," I agreed. She didn't want an apology, so I wouldn't give her one, and I wouldn't make her be the person to make me feel better after all of this. While I didn't choose to leave her there, it happened. It fucking sucked, but sometimes life happened that way. Sometimes there are no words. Nothing that can fix it or make it better.

But we can stop from making it worse.

"Do you want to watch a movie together, just me and you?"

She smiled, and for a second, there was light in her again. I knew it wouldn't last, but neither would the smothering claustrophobia and panic that was eating at her. Just like when we were kids, it would ease again, and while a part of her may change, my Moira was still there. She was stronger than this. Stronger than the shit life threw at us. We both were.

"Sure," she said.

We moved to the living room and settled in with a large plush throw blanket and grabbed some munchies.

Bandit curled in my lap and Moira leaned against me. If someone asked me, I couldn't tell them what we ended up watching. I don't think either of us were actually into it, but we stayed that way, the three of us huddled together, because we'd been through the wringer and come out alive.

The guys didn't come looking for me, and while we never spoke of it later, I appreciated it more than words could say.

CHAPTER 21

I RUBBED THE SLEEP OUT OF MY EYES AS I STUMBLED away from the couch and towards the bathroom. We'd fallen asleep there last night, bottle of wine, box of Oreos and all. Bandit grumbled as I moved away from him and pulled his lazy ass off the couch to trail after me. His paws scratched at my bare legs as he mewled.

"For fuck's sake," I muttered. Scooping him up, I made my way to the bathroom and redeposited him on the bathroom counter. Taking a piss with him on my lap wasn't happening, and it was too fucking early for me to deal with his crying if I left him in the hallway.

I made my way through my usual morning routine and started running a bath. Bandit decided that the shiny drawer knobs on the vanity were interesting enough to not wail about my ignoring him. I took care of my business while he spent two minutes opening and closing the drawer closest to him, absolutely fascinated by the way the light refracted off the metal knob. I was just rinsing my toothbrush when I saw something...

Why was there blue on my hand? I moved, turning my wrist to see a line of what looked like thin blue ivy-like vines running up my arm and disappearing under my shirt.

Holy Hell. What the fuck had happened to me?

I reached down and grasped the hem of the baggy white t-shirt. Did I want to see what was under this? I had been stabbed, after all. Well, it was there either way. May as well get it over with.

I lifted it over my head and flung it on the bathroom counter. Blue vines traveled up both my arms and across my chest, straight to where the pentagram sat snuggly between my breasts. It looked the same as before. Plain black. Unmoving. The vines swayed and crawled across my skin, down my belly and onto my legs. It was crazy that I hadn't noticed them before now and I was absolutely sure they weren't from the Horsemen.

A smoke-like skull was branded onto my belly. Its mouth was open at an odd angle. I squinted, moving closer to see. My fingers brushed over what looked like a textured edge and found it to be rough. The skin there was puckered with hardened scar tissue.

My stab wound, I realized. It was where I had been stabbed, and while I should have recognized that immediately, the scar was hardly noticeable between the brand and healing. Certainly, no longer a hole. Instead of something days or even weeks old, this could have been a scar from years ago. I wondered if that was my own natural healing now that I'd transitioned, or if Death's brand had done something. Altered me somehow.

I suppose only time would tell.

I brushed my hair behind both my shoulders to get a better look at the ivy creeping across my chest. It was kind of eerie, but also kind of sexy. Maybe these were from Lola?

I'd never heard of a demon with two brands, but what did I know? Not a whole hill of beans, apparently.

My eyes skipped over the rune left by the Unseelie woman and settled on something else. A discoloration of sorts around the curve of my neck where it attached to my jaw. I turned sideways and pulled my hair out of the way. Rysten's brand. It was white, so white that it actually stood out from my skin. His brand was a modified bio-hazard symbol with rings going through it. The whole thing couldn't be more than six or seven inches long, but it was really obvious once you knew it was there. While I didn't mind, I wondered if I should be having a talk with them about where I get branded. Otherwise Laran might try to brand his flaming Celtic knot on my forehead as a show of dominance.

If left to their own devices, they might start pissing on me to claim ownership, and the beast might come out and kick their asses again just to make it perfectly—and painfully—clear who was in charge.

Overall, it wasn't as bad as it could have been, and I didn't see a mark from Sin that could indicate it was the cause of my silence. That unsettled me even more, the lack of a mark despite her magic clearly being at play. I wasn't sure if it was better or worse that she hadn't left one. It was certainly well planned.

I turned away from the mirror and dipped one foot in the scalding hot water. Groaning in pleasure, I settled in. Just as my back hit the curved porcelain of the tub, a furry tail wrapped around my neck. I glanced over to see that Bandit had moved himself to act as my pillow. I sighed happily, content to sit here for the next hour until my skin was wrinkled and pruned.

Unfortunately, once again, fate had other plans.

Just as I started shaving my obscenely hairy legs, a doorbell rang. I didn't know we had a doorbell. Hell, I didn't even know where the front door was. The Horsemen had a knack for transporting me in and out by means of shadow walking, Pyroporting, or mirror walking. It seemed the one gift my transition hadn't given me was any form of teleporting, but if they had their way, they would carry me everywhere like I was some sort of invalid.

I continued shaving my legs, hoping, praying that whoever it was would go away, or that at the very least, I didn't need to get it.

The doorbell rang a second time.

"Ruby," Moira called. "Someone's at the door."

"No shit, Sherlock," I muttered as I finished my right leg. "Can't you get it?" I called back. A loud groan sounded from the living room.

"I can't move," Moira said. "I'm in a diabetic coma after all those Oreos." I rolled my eyes.

"It was only one bag," I griped. I'd seen her plow through two and a half before admitting defeat.

"But they were double stuffed," Moira mumbled, barely loud enough for me to hear.

"Oh, for Devil's sake." I set the razor aside and stood up, sloshing water all around the tub. Bandit leapt down and shook himself free of the water that doused him. I dried myself with a towel and pulled on the only bathrobe I saw. It was much slinkier than my own, and I grinned to myself in amusement. It was too large to be Moira's, and there was a price tag still on it. One of my mates had gone shopping and thought to buy me one. Judging by the slick, expensive material, I would guess Allistair.

I leaned down and scooped Bandit up, opening the bathroom door to wander back into the living room. The doorbell went off a third time.

In another room, I couldn't pinpoint which, someone rumbled a string of curses. A door opened and Laran appeared around the corner, wearing nothing but a pair of sweatpants. His golden skin shone in the morning light, and the fiery Celtic knot on his hip stood out against the black band of the sweats. His dark hair was pulled back to the base of his neck, the red tints flashing only briefly as he came to stand before me and angled his head.

"You don't usually wake until late morning," Laran said. His eyes roved to the "V" of my bathrobe where my brand sat. Those creeping blue vines moved beneath my skin, as if they sensed his presence and wanted to entangle him.

"Can you stop ogling each other and answer the fucking door," Moira grunted. She had one hand thrown across the back of the sofa haphazardly and her massive wings were spread at odd angles behind her.

"The others have it," Laran replied.

"What?"

Laran placed a hand on my lower back and led me around the kitchen to another hallway I hadn't noticed before. A stairway descended to a single entrance where I could only just make out a red bald head through the window above the door. The other three Horsemen crowded around the door as Julian pulled the knob to answer.

"Eugene?"

My rubrum friend looked up at me with a pained smile. He felt awkward. As usual, the guys were being assholes and didn't want him around because he had a dick. I rolled my eyes as I made my way down the stairs and weaved between them, *accidentally* brushing up against each of them as I went. I felt stares on my back as I stepped in front and looked up at Eugene.

"Hi Ruby," he mumbled as he blushed purple. "You're looking...well." His eyes purposely stayed on my face even though we both knew he wasn't interested in the lady bits beneath the robe. Finding some underwear beforehand might have been a better idea.

"Thanks, you too," I said kind of awkwardly.

Don't get me wrong. It was nice to see he made it out alive and all, but I wasn't sure why he'd shown up on my doorstep knowing how the Horsemen felt. I also couldn't figure out how much of our 'friendship' was real, and how much had been him playing into Donnach's hand. Did he know what his lover was capable of? Was he aware of how we'd been played? Maybe, this too, was a ruse.

Suddenly, I didn't feel quite as welcoming. That same paranoia that ate at Moira was beginning to wrap around me.

"Is there a reason for you being here?" Laran asked behind me, his thick arm wrapped around my waist and I knew he was glowering at him over my head. Eugene swallowed hard and thrust out the box he was holding.

"Donnach wanted to send his thanks." He lowered his eyes and Laran took the box since I was occupied holding Bandit.

"For the deal he emotionally manipulated me into?" I asked dryly.

"I—I don't know what to say." Me neither. "He created a weapon to help you...in Hell. It will only work for you."

That got my attention.

"We can take this from here," Allistair said coldly, cozying up to my other side. I was going to die of testosterone poisoning long before someone stabbed me again. That was for damn sure.

"Of course." Eugene turned to back away and fuck me if I didn't feel bad because he was sorry. I stepped forward begrudgingly.

"Wait—" I stood there, kind of awkwardly holding my hand out for him. I wasn't the hugging type, but after saving his soul and him sticking with me for five days, planted or not, I felt like that warranted more than a snide comment and dirty look. "Thank you, Eugene. For everything."

Eugene laced his hand in mine and shook it kindly, his eyes crinkling at the corners when he smiled. "And thank you, Ruby. If you ever need me—"

And apparently that was where the end of the Horsemen's patience fell. Laran yanked me inside and slammed the door on him.

"You guys are assholes!"

But I wasn't the least bit upset by it.

Allistair just shrugged, wrapping his long fingers around my elbow to steer me back up the stairs. I shook my head and chuckled.

"What was that?" Moira asked at the top of the stairs. We gathered around the kitchen island and Allistair handed me a cup of black coffee while Laran set the box down in front of me.

"I'm not sure..."

Taking a sip of my coffee, I tapped on my shoulder to motion for Bandit to move and he readjusted himself around me, slumping around my shoulders like a scarf. I gripped the edge of the box and opened it up.

"What is that?" Moira asked, letting out a kind of squeak.

"A gift," I replied as a smile started to spread across my face. Donnach had made me something special. I wondered if it was asking for forgiveness after manipulating me, or if it truly was a sign of thanks.

I hoped I'd never find out.

It was a crossbow of some sort, but small with a leather harness to strap it onto my arm. The contraption itself was made of a dark metal that was speckled yellow.

Bright red runes adorned the crossbow and a small white card sat on top.

To new beginnings, it read.

New beginnings, indeed.

I pulled it out and the beast smirked for the first time that day. She liked shiny things. She liked things that hurt. This was both, and it held all her attention.

"Do you even know how to use a crossbow?" Moira asked, raising a skeptically amused eyebrow. There were still shadows in her eyes, but not as pronounced. Last night had softened her some and hardened her in other ways.

We knew it wasn't going to be an easy journey.

"Nope, but I'm going to find out." My answer was met with several groans as I started to fidget with the small contraption. A large hand settled over mine and I looked up at Laran.

"We need to check this out before you can use it," he said in complete seriousness. Part of me wanted to be a child and ask why, but the adult in me told that bitch to shut up.

Yes, it was a cool toy. No, I could not afford to drop my guard just because Donnach hadn't tried to kill me directly. He was still responsible for some unforgivable shit, whether he knew I realized it or not.

I relinquished my hold on the crossbow to Laran, so he and Allistair could examine it.

"There's a card at the bottom," Moira said. She reached into the empty box to pull out a white envelope. "To Ruby Morningstar, you have returned. We look forward to meeting you," Moira read aloud.

Laran froze beside me and the rest of the Horsemen narrowed in on the letter in her hand. This didn't sound like it was from Donnach.

Ummmm... "Does it say who it's signed by?" I asked.

Moira turned the slip of paper over and her face paled. Fingers slightly twitching, she reached out and showed me the card.

The Six Sins.

Laran peered at it over my shoulder and let out a string of curses. "Damnit, Julian—they know—the Sins know." As soon as Laran said it, Julian went quiet and Allistair let out a deep, semi-dramatic sigh.

"We knew this was coming, Death. We can't hide her here forever. It was only a matter of time once word reached Hell and we had a deal," Allistair said.

"What are you talking about?" Moira asked, her voice rising with tension. She reached out for my hand, and I couldn't tell if she realized the glass wall had just warbled.

"The Six Sins have summoned her, and as the heir, she has to answer their call," Julian answered.

He had fallen into a resigned state over this like the flip of a switch, and with us no longer blood bound, he masked his features carefully. Not that his attempts kept it all from me. His emotions were bleeding out. Worry. Anxiety. Nothing so close as to make me think I was a dead woman, but certainly enough to know this wasn't great.

"Well, I guess that answers my next question. Looks like we're going to Hell," I said with a grim realization. It was true. This was actually happening. I would go to

Hell and meet the Sins, even if they were members of my father's former harem. That wouldn't stop me from doing what I had to do.

Sure, I still had a lot to learn and not a lot of time. My enemies were out there, and if Moira and I were right—some were closer to us than anyone realized.

But. I was alive. I was breathing. I had both my familiars safe and sound, and the strength of my four mates behind me. I was about as close to ready as this heir to Hell was ever going to get.

And this time, I was playing for keeps.

This time...I was going for my crown, and no one, not even the Six Sins, would stop me.

EPILOGUE

She stepped onto the ledge, nothing more than a shadow in the night. The wind had died down and the skies calmed for the time, but a storm was coming. A storm whose outcome would last many lifetimes.

She stared at the young girl, Lucifer's daughter. Her eyes were blue like his, but she looked like her mother. Every bit as beautiful as the Deadly Sin of Lust. If the girl proved to have half her cunning and none of her father's ego, they might actually win this game. *Might.*

"Having second thoughts, Sinumpa?" the voice said from behind her. A dark Seelie man with red runes upon his skin stepped up on the ledge. They watched the girl and her guardians from afar, just as Sin had always watched her.

"No. I will do what must be done," she said with a determined hush that whispered over the sleeping city.

"And compelling my lover; was that part of what had

to be done?" the man asked, an edge of spite in his tone, but he knew better than to push it.

"Her mind was too strong for me to get her straight to you. The rubrum's was easier. More pliant. We've been over this. You know why I chose him. Don't tell me you are growing a heart now." She inclined her face toward him and raised a single white eyebrow. Her mercury eyes bore into his with secrets that even the old Fae did not and could not possibly know.

"No," he relented. "But you almost showed your hand. The green one is onto you, and she does not have the distraction of four lovers to stop her from seeking."

"The green one doesn't possess enough information. As it was, Ruby needed the push," Sin replied. Like a lone wolf, she had stalked this child for twenty-three years. Always waiting in the shadows. Always watching. Not even her master knew that she had followed Lola and the girl many years ago, that she had kept tabs long before Satan's fall.

Her master was powerful and cunning in her own right, but Sin had been planning her freedom for many years now. She had learned from the best.

Beside her, the Seelie man snorted. "You made her think her familiar was dead. She could have destroyed the city if you'd made that spell any stronger. She only felt an echo of the loss of losing a familiar. One of your riskier moves, that was. I don't disagree with it, but it was dangerous."

"She is not one to break easily. I needed something to unite them and spur her into action. Without that, your sister would still be trapped down there, need I remind you." She didn't look at him, but he cut his eyes sideways, pursing his lips in annoyance.

"They would have come for her familiars eventually, and Morvaen would have dealt. She was punished for her disobedience, and now I have four Seelie who are willing to attest to the girl's morals. It's a win-win, the way I see it. She will have allies to usurp her father's killer, and we will have the chance to return home."

He clenched his fist in strength, turning his attention back to the blue-haired woman. She had the gauntlet crossbow attached to her arm. It fit perfectly, but that was no surprise. He'd used her hair to craft her something that would be exclusively hers. It would never miss. It would never run out of arrows. She would never lose it.

The magic that went into its creation was a small price to pay for what the young queen would bring him. It was an apology, for what he and the white-haired woman had done to her. What they would do to her, to see their ends met.

"Return home..." Sin paused, drawing his attention back to her. "Do you still wish to return home after all this time? Hell is not what you once thought it."

The man went quiet as the night sat around them. The air stagnant, but not quite stifling. He truly hated this world and the limitations it brought.

"Anything is better than here, where I feel my immortality slowly leeching away. This land does not like magic..." he trailed off, examining the fine wrinkles that had begun to form on his hands. Five thousand years. That's how long he had walked this earth.

But age was catching up with him. After so long, one

might think he was ready for what came next, but all the ancient Fae wished was to return home. It had been far too long.

"The time is coming. The Sins have called upon her, and even Death knows better than to resist their summons. She will be tested, and should she survive, they will back her. It won't be long now, Donnach." Sin clasped a hand on the elder Fae's shoulder and he did the same to her. It was a sign of respect; a parting of ways, similar to goodbye, but not so informal.

"She must survive. The fate of the worlds depends upon it." A sliver of his age and desperation leaked through into his voice. He had held on for thousands of years, just for this moment. He wouldn't lose it now because of the Sins and their games.

"Ready your people, friend. I will watch over her."

As she always had.

But she looked forward to the day the only back she had to watch was her own.

Freedom was so close. One wrong step would send it all up in flames.

She wouldn't allow that. She couldn't.

The Seelie man tipped his head to her and Sin disappeared into the night. In the blink of an eye, her white hair vanished, leaving nothing more than a flowery scent she could not rid herself of, although she had tried many times.

Donnach turned back and looked across the street through a glass wall while Ruby and her protectors remained oblivious to the Fae watching over them. She was young and inexperienced, but she was also his only hope.

Because in this deadly game of chess, everyone knew the most powerful piece on the board was the Queen.

To be continued...

Join Kel's newsletter at kelcarpenter.com to find out more about the next book in the Queen of the Damned series, Brimstone Nightmares.

ALSO BY KEL CARPENTER

The Daizlei Academy Series:

Heir of Shadows (Book One)
Trial by Heist (Novella)
Scion of Midnight (Book Two)
Queen of Lies (Book Three)
Untitled (Coming Soon)

Queen of the Damned Series:

Lucifer's Daughter (Book One)
Wicked Games (Book Two)
Infernal Desires (Book Three)
Brimstone Nightmares (Coming Soon)

ABOUT THE AUTHOR

Kel Carpenter is a USA Today Bestselling Author and writer of all things fantasy. She loves reading, watching Netflix original shows, and subjecting her favorite co-author and editor to crazy, harebrained book ideas. Kel currently resides in Atlanta, GA with her boyfriend and three fur-children. When she is not writing or working on completing her senior year of college, she is spending time with her dog, Harley, or teasing her two cats with a laser pointer.

Join Kel's Readers Group!

ACKNOWLEDGMENTS

I acknowledge no one but myself. Good job, me. You really fucked this one up.

Made in the USA
Lexington, KY
13 August 2018